Books by Anina Collins

The Eleventh Hour (Poppy McGuire Mysteries #1)
After Hours (Poppy McGuire Mysteries #2)
Top of the Hour (Poppy McGuire Mysteries #3)

THE ELEVENTH HOUR

ANINA COLLINS

The Eleventh Hour

Poppy McGuire has always been a curious soul, but it's her life that's usually the topic of conversation in the small town of Sunset Ridge. But now one of the town's most important citizens has been found murdered, and everyone's life is suspect.

What begins as a friendly wager with her old friend Officer Derek Hampton soon becomes far more for Poppy, and she turns to Alex Montero for help, but the enigmatic former Baltimore cop's quiet way hides as many secrets as each suspect they encounter.

Everyone in Sunset Ridge has something to hide, but Poppy and Alex are determined to uncover the identity of the murderer. They just have to watch that they don't become the next victims.

Chapter One

THE TOWN OF Sunset Ridge hadn't had a murder in almost a decade. Well, that wasn't exactly the truth, but the town's leaders had done everything in their power to make it seem like it was. In the world of small towns, perception is everything.

The awful whining sound of a Sunset Ridge police car's siren jarred me out of a daydream about that trip to Ireland I kept promising myself I'd take, and I sat bolt upright in my kitchen chair as the thought that something terrible had happened to my father tore through my brain. Still groggy since I hadn't had my first cup of morning coffee yet, I reached for my cell phone and called him. As usual, he answered in that casual way of his.

"It's a little early to be calling, isn't it, honey?"

"I heard a siren and just wanted to check that everything's okay," I said as relief washed over me.

"I'm okay, honey. It's probably just Derek overreacting to some traffic issue."

Looking out my kitchen window, I saw the first rays of the sun just beginning to peek up over the horizon. "It's a little early for Derek to be using the siren for something as small as a traffic stop, Dad. I wonder what happened."

My father chuckled low and deep in a way that reminded me of when he used to play Santa at Christmastime when I was a little girl. "Well, now that you know I'm okay, you can go find out what's going on. Just remember our chief isn't a fan of you poking your nose around in the police department's cases, Poppy. The last time he caught you I heard about it at the bar for weeks."

"Don't worry about it, Dad. I'm a grown woman, and Dominick doesn't scare me. He hasn't since the sixth grade when he pulled my hair on the way home from school and I punched him straight in the nose."

Another chuckle and then my father gave me his usual warning when he knew I was about to go investigating. "Just be careful, Elizabeth. Even in Sunset Ridge, there are bad people."

I couldn't help but roll my eyes at his words. Whenever he called me by my given name instead of the nickname everyone usually used, I knew he was serious. To him, I was perpetually that sixth grade girl who had to be talked into defending herself against Dominick Hampton.

But I wasn't that girl anymore. After thirty-one years, I'd met my fair share of good and bad people. In fact, if my father knew even a fraction of what I'd seen, he likely would have done everything in his power to force me to move in with him in that place of his above the bar he ran a few blocks away.

"Yes, Dad. Don't worry. I'll make sure to keep my eyes open and my nose clean."

"Good. Will I see you later tonight? You haven't been by the bar in a few weeks."

Standing from the table, I peered out my window that overlooked my backyard and gave me a good look at the houses on the next street. Seeing nothing but the usual early morning comings and goings, I headed toward the dish drainer next to the sink to grab my coffee mug and begin my day.

"Maybe. Who knows? I might find something interesting was going on with that siren. I'll talk to you later, Dad. I'm happy to hear you're okay."

"Always, honey. You don't have to worry about me going anywhere anytime soon. You're stuck with me for a long time."

The thought of my father not being around settled into my brain and a lump formed in my throat. Pushing it down, I forced myself to stay cheery. "I love you, Dad. Talk to you later."

"I love you, Poppy. Be careful."

I pressed END and set my cell phone down on the kitchen countertop to get my morning coffee going. While I absentmindedly went through the steps needed for coffee to appear in my mug, I tried to push the upsetting idea of my father dying out of my head. I knew it was irrational, but since my mother's death, I worried about him.

Not that he was on death's doorstep. Nowhere close. For a man in his fifties, he acted more like a twenty-something. Some days he could be found hiking in the mountains just outside of town, and then other times he'd join the neighborhood kids in a pickup basketball game at the park near the bar.

Joe McGuire definitely had a lot of years left. It was just the loss of my mother that made me forget that sometimes. Worrying about him had become my avocation over the years to the point of giving up the chance for a future with a few boyfriends I cared about in favor of staying in Sunset Ridge near my father.

I didn't regret my choices so much as wonder if I'd really made them for the reasons I believed. Such were the thoughts that settled into my brain as I leaned against the gold Formica countertop in my kitchen sipping my morning dose of the nectar of the gods. They may have craved ambrosia, but for me, coffee was that perfect drink that gave me what I needed to start my day.

My first cup finished, I headed off toward the shower to get ready to check out the reason for Derek's siren before I started work for the day.

THE GROUNDS, THE coffee shop nearest to *The Sunset Eagle* newspaper offices, bustled with customers flowing in to get their morning drink. A local version of the far more popular coffee shops the town council had decided couldn't do business within city limits, The Grounds served the most delicious pastries I'd ever tasted, in addition to coffee and tea. I blamed the owners, Pam and Gerald Branch, for the ten pounds I'd gained in the past year because of their heavenly danish that literally melted on the tongue. I needed more will power and less danish, if the feel of my skirt around my waist was any indication.

Standing fourth in line, I checked my phone for any messages and heard the morning's gossip. Unlike the usual whispers about what had happened at the town council meeting or who had been seen the night before at Diamanti's, the best restaurant in town, today's gossip was all about something that hadn't occurred in Sunset Ridge in nearly a decade.

Murder.

But whose? I leaned closer to the man in front of me, close enough to smell the remnants of his menthol shaving cream he'd used as he got ready that morning, and heard the words "strangled right in her own home."

I tapped him on the shoulder, surprising him out of his whispering to the woman next to him, and he turned around with wide eyes to look at me. Before he could say anything, I asked, "Who was strangled?"

"You're Poppy McGuire, aren't you?" he asked as he searched my face. "I remember you from school."

Not really interested in taking a stroll down memory lane with whoever he was, I smiled and nodded. "Was someone in town strangled?"

"Yes," he answered as the line inched forward toward the counter. "Geneva Woodward was found strangled in her home not an hour ago. We assumed it was just Derek indiscriminately using that damn siren again, but this time he wasn't crying wolf. A murder in Sunset Ridge. It's been so long, I'm not even sure the cops will know what to do."

A murder in Sunset Ridge! The hairs on the back of my neck stood at attention as a chill raced down my spine. The sleepy little hamlet of Sunset Ridge had very little crime, much less murder. It was the type of place where people still left their doors unlocked when they went to bed at night. My hometown always seemed like someplace straight out of Norman Rockwell's paintings—the kind of Americana that people on the coasts insisted didn't exist anymore, if it ever had.

Lost in the news that a murder had been committed

right there in what was thought to be our tight-knit community, I didn't see it was my turn to order until the woman behind me gently nudged my shoulder.

"You're up, sweetie."

I gave the elderly woman with the steel grey hair a meek smile and stepped up to the counter to speak to Jennie, the morning cashier at The Grounds. A student at one of the local community colleges, she had been the person who served me my second cup of morning coffee every Monday through Friday for the past four years. We'd talked a few times about my job as an investigative journalist for The Bottom Line, so I wasn't surprised when she leaned toward me and in a tone full of curiosity asked, "Are you on your way to the murder scene? It's all anyone can talk about since we first heard about it."

Smiling, I nodded, happy to give her the idea that I was better connected than I actually was. In truth, while Derek might not have a problem letting me poke my nose into his newest and biggest case ever, his brother and the police chief Dominick would likely clap the cuffs on me if he caught me within twenty yards of the crime scene.

But I'd try anyway.

I handed Jennie five dollars and told her to keep the change before grabbing my danish and coffee and turning on my heels to head the three blocks north toward Geneva Woodward's home in the ritzy section of town where the houses were finer and more distinguished than the rest of Sunset Ridge.

And the residents who lived in them were like local royalty.

The crowd of people standing on the sidewalk in

front of Geneva's sprawling blue and white Queen Anne Victorian home grew by the minute with neighbors rubbernecking to get a look at the scene of death inside. I pushed my way through mothers stopped on their way to school with their children, old ladies with little dogs in their arms, and a few elderly men who'd paused in their morning walk to give their opinion on how wealthy people lived differently than the rest of us.

I approached Craig, the man who occupied the lowest rung on the Sunset Ridge police force ladder. Three years younger than me, he'd always harbored a not-so-secret crush for me since high school. He stood under six foot and was thin, which gave him a slight appearance, but big blue eyes never failed to charm the onlookers he usually was charged to control.

"Hi Poppy," he said with a big, boyish smile. "I guess you heard about all the excitement. Everyone's pretty much gone now, but Derek's still inside with the coroner."

Looking past him, I scanned the house's wrap-around porch for anyone else that might be there. "Dominick around?"

Craig's smile grew bigger, and he shook his head. "Nope. You're in the clear."

I patted him on the shoulder as I walked by. "Thanks, Craig. Watch these people. This is the biggest news since that town council meeting when Derek had to arrest that streaker last year."

He threw his head back and laughed, likely remembering how the policeman looked chasing after a naked and wrinkly old man running through council chambers yelling about how the hike in taxes would steal the clothes off his back.

"I'm on the job. Good to see you again, Poppy."

I waved back at him and smiled, flattered as always by his crush on me. Climbing the five wooden steps up to Geneva's porch, I wondered what a strangulation looked like. I'd never seen a murder victim in person, so I stopped a moment at the front door to take a deep breath and prepare for what might await me inside.

Derek spied me there and walked over shaking his head. "I should have known you'd show up. Are you here as an investigative journalist for The Bottom Line or as the writer of the society page for *The Sunset Ridge Eagle*?"

Tilting my chin up, I leveled my gaze on Derek Hampton's attractive face. A friend of my family's since I was a little girl, he had grown into the kind of man who just had to be in law enforcement. Tall, muscular, and strong, he still looked like the star football player he'd been back in high school over a decade ago. But he'd always been more jock than brain, so despite having dreamy brown eyes the color of dark chocolate and beautiful, oh-so-touchable wavy brown hair, he and I had always been nothing more than friends.

"I admit my work for The Bottom Line is pretty much just collecting gossip, Derek, but give me some credit for being a decent human being. Anyway, Geneva Woodward isn't anyone the site's fans would care about. They prefer a different crowd. And it's a little ghoulish for me to be here as the society page writer, don't you think?"

He thought about what I'd said for a long moment, shrugged, and flashed me one of his trademark flirty grins. "Then you're here because you can't keep yourself away from me? Any chance you brought me my favorite danish?"

I rolled my eyes. "Really? You've got a dead woman inside and you're going for hitting on me?"

Derek stepped aside to show me Geneva Woodward lying on her hardwood floor not ten feet away. "She doesn't care."

Walking past him toward where Geneva lay, I chastised him for being a smart ass. "A little decorum, Derek. A woman's been murdered."

He followed behind me as I made my way into the elegantly decorated formal dining room. Although a body lay on the floor, my eyes couldn't help scanning everything else around me. A crystal chandelier hung from the ceiling above, surrounded by a decorative plaster medallion with an Old World scroll pattern. The walls were covered in a gold and cream colored velvet flocked wallpaper so indicative of the Victorian Era and the kind that always seemed to have a hidden terrifying face in the pattern. On the hardwood floor underneath a heavy cherry wood dining set lay a decorative rug of burgundy and cream.

And Geneva dead, her long blond hair spread out around her head like a halo and a pained, shocked expression permanently etched into her fine features.

"Someone strangled her with one of her own scarves," Derek explained as he tried to direct my attention away from the décor.

I looked down at her there near my feet and recognized the bright red scarf around her neck. "I saw her wearing that one night at Diamanti's. It's expensive."

Derek swiveled his head back and forth to look at the room that surrounded us. "Would you expect anything less from the look of this place?"

Geneva Woodward had inherited her family's money that went back all the way to before the Civil War. It had long been rumored the Woodward fortune came from bootlegging whisky in the nearby mountains, despite the airs the family had always put on around town. When Geneva's parents died months apart nearly twenty years ago, she'd come into millions, along with the upscale Victorian home I stood in and various vacation homes around the world she never used.

Shaking my head to answer his question, I secretly admitted to myself that I'd been jealous of Geneva more than once. Wealthy, beautiful, and able to live a life of indolent luxury, she seemed to have everything without having to work a day for it.

"You ever been in here before today?" Derek asked. "I always figured it would look more like a museum."

Sidestepping his question, I asked a few of my own in Gatling gun fashion. "How long is she dead? Did the killer take anything? Was this a robbery too? Did they break in?"

He stepped back, almost as if he felt under attack by my rapid fire questioning, and then he answered each one in succession. "The coroner guesses she died late last night. We don't know if anything is missing yet. It could take weeks to inventory everything in this house. She had what looks like a million things in here, and they all appear priceless. But right now, we're considering this a murder only. And no, there was no forcible entry."

I looked around the room and into the next room, a conservatory of some sort, as his answers settled into my brain. "Who would do this to her?" I mumbled, not really looking for him to answer me.

"Someone who wanted her dead. Now if we're done here, I need to let the coroner take her body for an autopsy to make sure it was strangulation."

Nodding, I took one last look around and my gaze settled on her right hand, unusually bare. "Derek, where are her rings? Geneva was known for wearing her rings, and they were worth a fortune. I remember hearing the diamond itself was more than two carats, and that ruby one of hers could be seen on her from across the street."

He shrugged. "There were no rings on her fingers when I got here, and I was the first one on the scene. Maybe she took them off when she was at home."

I took one last look around and nodded. "Maybe. Well, thanks for letting me in, Derek. Time to go to work."

As I headed toward the front door, I heard him complain, "So I'm not going to get that danish after all? I might just have to start restricting you from my crime scenes, Poppy."

Knowing he likely wouldn't do anything of the sort, I still dropped the bag with the cheese danish on the table in the foyer before I left. Friends willing to break the rules needed to be kept happy.

THE CROWD WHISPERING and gossiping in front of Geneva's house was nothing compared to that of the *Sunset Eagle* employees that morning. By the time I got to my desk, I'd heard no fewer than eight people share their opinion of what had happened to poor Geneva. Hoping to block them out and get to work, I closed the door behind me and settled in to get started with my day.

A knock less than five minutes later told me that might be easier said than done. Before I could tell whoever it was that I was busy, I saw Bethany Lewis peek her blond head in through the crack in the door.

"Did you hear about what happened to Geneva Woodward? It's all anyone can talk about this morning."

Bethany was the closest thing to a best friend for me, so I waved her in and told her to close the door behind her. She worked in advertising sales for the newspaper and since she was near my age, we'd become close in the years we'd worked together at *The Eagle*.

She sat down in the chair beside my desk and said in a voice full of excitement, "A murder in Sunset Ridge! Can you believe it?"

"I stopped by her house on my way here and saw her. Someone strangled her with one of her scarves. You know, the fancy ones she always wore."

Bethany's blue eyes grew as big as saucers and her mouth dropped open in shock. "Strangled? I can't believe it."

"And you know what was just as odd? She didn't have any of her rings on," I said, hoping to find out if I was the only one who thought that fact was strange.

"She was at home, so maybe she didn't wear them there. I don't wear any rings at home. I always take them off when I get home from work."

Chuckling, I said, "Derek said the same thing. I guess I just have a fixation with her rings. She was always wearing such huge stones, and I never could understand why. They were so gaudy."

Bethany wiggled her right hand with rings on the middle three fingers in front of my face and smiled. "Because they're pretty. Women love rings, Poppy.

You're the exception to that, of course."

I spread out my ringless fingers over my laptop and looked down at the bareness of them before I turned back toward Bethany. "I guess I am."

"So do they have any suspects? I can't believe it. There's likely a murderer right here in Sunset Ridge walking amongst us."

As we talked about how snobby Geneva had always been toward virtually everyone in town, I wondered if I knew her murderer. Strangulation was personal. Unlike killing with a gun, strangling someone required being right next to them as they took their last breath and left this world.

Who in Sunset Ridge had gotten that close to Geneva Woodward that they'd be welcome in her house and hate her enough to want to kill her in such an intimate way?

THREE HOURS AND very little work accomplished later, I walked to the Sunset Ridge police station to find Derek and see if he'd uncovered anything more about Geneva's murder. I found him sitting in his tan upholstered office chair staring off into space like he was deep in thought.

"Hey, you. How goes the case?"

He turned to look at me and for a moment seemed like he couldn't figure out why on earth I'd be leaning against the doorframe to his office. Then, as if a light was switched on in his brain, he smiled and shook his head.

"It doesn't. You wouldn't be here to tell me you know who did it, would you?"

I stepped into his beige office and took a seat in one

of the two black plastic chairs he kept in front of his desk. For a moment, I studied the plain walls with not even a plaque or a picture on them and shook my head.

"No. I was just curious to know if you had made any headway."

Derek sighed and tossed a file folder off to the side. "Nope. We found dozens of fingerprints in that room, but none of them are…" He stopped talking and blew the air out of his lungs slowly.

"I've never seen you so frustrated, Derek. What's going on here?"

He pinched the bridge of his nose and sighed again. "My fellow officers loped through my crime scene without even thinking of wearing gloves. I swear to God they live to make my life harder."

"You know they mean no harm. It's just that they're used to rescuing cats from trees and writing tickets for parking violations."

"I know. It's just that I have no suspects and I'm not even sure where to begin. Geneva made plenty of enemies in Sunset Ridge, but none of them really appear capable of murder."

I couldn't help but smile at Derek's naiveté. "Of course they're capable of murder. Anyone is. How is it you're a policeman again?"

"Asks the social events reporter for the local newspaper," he teased back. "You seem to forget that Sunset Ridge hasn't had a murder committed since before I came onto the force. Murders don't happen here, Poppy."

"It looks like they do now, and this one is personal."

Derek narrowed his eyes skeptically. "Why would you think that?"

"It's simple. To kill someone like this, the murderer had to be close to her. Whoever killed Geneva was let into her house since you said there was no forcible entry, and she let them close enough to her that they could tighten that scarf around her neck and choke the life out of her. Look who we're talking about here, Derek. Geneva was icy on her best days. Most of the time she looked at those of us who lived in the same town as her like we were underlings or peons. Like we were beneath her. That tells me this was personal."

"You've been watching too many Lifetime movies, Poppy. With all the stuff in Geneva's house, I think it's just as likely this was a robbery gone bad. Probably somebody passing through who cased out her house and saw a gold mine."

I wasn't surprised to hear this come from him. Derek was never the sharpest tool in the shed, and I could understand him not wanting to deal with a murder if it could be a robbery that had gone wrong just as easily.

But that didn't mean I had to agree with him.

"I'll tell you what. Since we clearly aren't going to agree, what do you say we both investigate Geneva's murder? You guys only have a handful of full time cops to use on this case, and you know it. This isn't exactly the DC police department, so you can use all the help you can get."

Sunset Ridge had gotten some special dispensation from someone important when the town was founded to have its own police department, unlike other towns in the state, but it had the ability to bring in the State Police, if it needed to. I knew Dominick wouldn't want that kind of help taking over a case so important to the town, even if his brother would gladly welcome the support, which meant Derek was going to remain shorthanded.

"I'll poke around and see what I can find from the potential pool of local murderers while you guys check out your idea that it was someone from outside of town who only wanted to rob her."

"And I would let you do this why?" he asked with a mischievous smile.

"Because I can help. I promise whatever I find out I'll tell you so it won't be like I'm conducting my own investigation. I'll just be asking some questions. That's all. Think of me like someone you've deputized to help you since a police force this size isn't exactly set up to deal with crimes like murder on top of the dozens of other calls you get every day, and you know those aren't going to stop just because Geneva Woodward was found dead."

Threading his fingers behind his head, he asked, "And you think people are going to talk to you about this?"

"Of course they will. I'm well-known in town and I work for the newspaper. People love talking to me, Derek. Even you do. I just got you to agree to let me help on this case."

He shook his head as his face grew serious. "Not so fast. Even if I wanted to agree to this crazy idea, and I'm not sure I do, the chief of police would lose his mind if he heard about it. You know how he gets when you stop in to just see crime scenes. He'd have my head if he found out I was letting you do this."

Leaning across his desk, I extended my hand to shake his. "Then we don't let him find out. Agreed?"

"I'm not sure, Poppy. This isn't an ordinary case.

Everything's got to be done by the book, and I'm pretty sure that doesn't involve letting you snoop around."

For one of the few times in all the years I'd known Derek, I sensed a real reluctance in him to give me what I wanted. I'd have to lay it on thick. "Come on. I can help and you know it. Just take a chance this one time. Who knows? I might find the one clue you need to crack this case wide open. Imagine how happy the chief would be if you were the one to solve the murder of one of Sunset Ridge's most important citizens. Sounds like bragging rights in the Hampton family to me. Maybe even a commendation from the town council."

Derek looked down at my hand grasping his and took a deep breath in. Blowing the air out slowly, he shook his head. "Don't make me regret this, Poppy."

"We just crossed the Rubicon, Derek. No regrets."

"I don't know what that means, but just don't make this come back to haunt me, okay?"

I winked and flashed him a smile as inside I bubbled with excitement. "Not to worry. By the time this case is solved, you're going to wonder what you ever did without me."

Turning to leave, I saw the police chief standing in the doorway. Nearly his brother's twin, except for his hair that was a slightly lighter shade of brown, Dominick stared at me with a curious look in his eyes. "Good morning, Poppy. What are you doing here?"

"Just came by to tell your brother about the streetlight outside my house. It burnt out the other night, so I figured I'd get him on the case," I lied as I brushed past him before he could ask any more questions. "Thanks for getting that fixed, Derek!"

And with that, I left to begin my investigation of who killed Geneva Woodward.

Chapter Two

I LEFT THE police station practically walking on air and my mind racing with where to begin. Derek had been right about Geneva. She had made a fair number of enemies in Sunset Ridge, and I believed any one of them could be a cold-blooded murderer. All I had to do was pick a starting point and go from there.

As I walked down Main Street I remembered hearing somewhere that often murder begins close at home, so I pointed myself in the direction of Geneva's house three blocks away. She may have been standoffish most of the time, but I was willing to bet Geneva's neighbors might know something about who she may have let get close enough to her to kill her.

Her nearest neighbor in the house next to hers was a woman named Michelle Steadman. In her forties, like Geneva, she could usually be seen around town with bags filled with her almost daily purchases. No one liked to shop like Michelle.

I remembered my father telling me about Michelle divorcing yet another husband a few years ago. She'd been through three, at last count, and my father said this last one had left her a very wealthy woman.

But Michelle was new money, and old money like

Geneva rarely appreciated the insta-wealth of people like her neighbor one house to the left.

Unlike the Woodward home, Michelle Steadman's didn't present itself as the perfect Victorian. The front stairs were a few years past the need for a fresh coat of paint, and as I knocked on the front door, I saw through the panes of glass flanking it that the inside had a less impressive look to it too. Michelle hobbled her way toward me on her heels with freshly manicured toenails and flashed me a big grin as she opened the door.

"Hi! Can I help you?" she asked in a very chipper voice for someone who lived next to a house where a murder had just occurred less than twenty-four hours before.

"Michelle, my name is Poppy McGuire. I was wondering if you'd be willing to talk to me about Geneva Woodward."

For a moment, it looked like she wanted to tell me to go away, but then she flashed me another toothy grin and opened the door wide for me to walk inside. "Sure. Come on in."

Small town trust ran deep, at least with her, it seemed. Her next door neighbor had just been murdered, and she was letting strangers in with little hesitation. I waited for her to close the door, and she joined me in the vast foyer.

"Let's go into the parlor. Would you like anything to drink? I can make a fresh pitcher of lemonade, if you like," she said as she showed me to a room with high ceilings like in Geneva's home, but noticeably less opulent. There were no finely crafted medallions or flocked velvet wallpaper in this home.

Extending her arm toward a vivid blue upholstered

sofa, she said, "Please, join me on the settee and we can talk about poor, poor Geneva."

I'd never heard Geneva described with that adjective, and as I took my seat next to Michelle, I sensed a tone of almost celebration in her voice.

"I was wondering if you and Geneva were close. You were next door neighbors with so much in common, including you both having gorgeous homes in the finer section of town."

While the words flowed out of my mouth, I worried Michelle might see me as more sycophant than someone looking for real answers, but my concern was all for nothing. Michelle Steadman, like most women of means, adored hearing compliments on her possessions and began to explain her relationship to poor Geneva in detail without any more prodding from me.

"Oh, it's so terrible about what happened to poor Geneva. She was such a dear. We only just met three years ago when I bought this house, but we became instant best friends since we had so much in common."

"Michelle, do you know of any problems she might have been having?"

She reached out and gave my forearm a gentle squeeze. "Oh, please call me Shelley. May I call you Poppy, Ms. McGuire? You know, I've read your society column in the paper many times. You always write such interesting stories."

"Shelley, thank you so much. I'm so flattered that you enjoy my work. And yes, please call me Poppy."

In truth, what I wrote for *The Sunset Ridge Eagle* was little more than fluff meant to make the most important people in town feel even more important. I'd tried to include some real pieces on local issues only to have my boss at the paper, the rarely friendly Mr. Howard Fleming, tell me that my job was to simply report on the most influential in Sunset Ridge society and nothing else. So I'd done nothing else ever since.

That Shelley enjoyed my stories was because she'd appeared in them a good number of times since coming into her newfound money after divorcing husband number three. Her taste in writing was at the very least skewed by her vanity.

"Poppy, I wish I knew what happened. Geneva and I were very close. You know, we had so much in common. Two wealthy single women in a town where virtually everyone was with someone and most married. You must know what I mean."

Shelley's reference to my single status in a place where being married seemed to be the principal aim of most the residents made me want to roll my eyes. I'd accepted my choices in staying in Sunset Ridge to be near my father, even if it meant a distinct lack of potential husbands I had any interest in.

"She and I both loved nice things." Pointing toward art that hung on the far wall of the parlor, she beamed her pride at her possession. "Do you see that painting there? I bought it six months ago for nearly ten thousand dollars. I had it appraised the other day and the delightful man told me he believed I could sell it for nearly five thousand more than I bought it for."

I glanced at the painting and didn't recognize it as anything noteworthy from the few art history classes I'd taken in college. A woman with a vase standing in front of a giraffe didn't seem like anything that would be considered stellar in the art world, but I was no art aficionado, so it could have been worth all the money

Shelley had paid for it.

Before I could fake my appreciation for her picture, she directed my attention to a table in the opposite corner of the room. Ornate and finely crafted in dark wood, its legs curled up on the bottoms into a scrolled form. Unlike the painting, I could see that piece of furniture being worth something.

"I got that table right after moving in here. I saw one just like it in Geneva's house and had to have one of my own," Shelley said with a satisfied smile.

"It's lovely. You and Geneva certainly have wonderful taste."

Correcting me, Shelley nodded and frowned. "Had. Poor Geneva. I just can't believe what happened. I'm going to miss her so much. We spent so much time together."

As she went on and on about how close they were, I thought about how often Geneva frequented Diamanti's across the street from my father's bar and how I'd never seen her with Shelley on any of the three or four nights a week she ate dinner at the restaurant. For people who were such good friends, it seemed odd that they'd never eaten together.

"You spent a lot of time together? I have to admit I didn't really know her," I said, hoping to glean something from Shelley other than more cataloguing of her acquisitions.

"Oh, yes! We saw each other every day. I remember the day I met her. The moving van had just pulled away and she was standing on her porch looking over at my house, probably wondering if someone like her had moved in. She gave me a smile, so I immediately went over to introduce myself."

Stifling a laugh, I imagined Geneva standing the way she usually did, arms folded across her chest and her back straight as a board like some matron in charge of a strict boarding school. The thought she had when she saw Shelley and her new money move in next door was likely something far closer to disgust than interest.

"I think many in town thought of her as a little cool," I said gingerly, trying not to tip my hand about how little I believed in this close friendship Shelley continued to claim.

She nodded. "She was. Even that first day when I introduced myself, Geneva wasn't as friendly as I'd hoped. And she could be quite difficult. That's true too. Why just last week she was a real bi—"

Shelley stopped herself and plastered a smile onto her lips. "It's not nice to speak ill of the dead. For whatever she was, Geneva is no more."

Now it was my time to squeeze her arm. "Of course. Respect is all we mean here."

Satisfied that she hadn't besmirched poor Geneva's reputation by calling her a bitch, Shelley leaned in close to me.

"She wasn't always so chilly, though, if you know what I mean."

For a moment, I didn't know if Shelley had just come out to me or if she meant Geneva had a boyfriend. Always single, she had long been assumed to be just the latest in old maids from the Woodward family. The gossip around town was that some ancestor way back in her family tree had cursed all the daughters born into the Woodward name to be alone forever. Even though it was very likely nonsense, it certainly made for interesting whispers whenever Geneva was seen in town, although I doubted the town busybodies disapproved of her marital status like they did mine because she was loaded. As in most places, money talked in Sunset Ridge.

"Do you mean she was seeing someone?" I asked, hoping Shelley's need for propriety had been just temporary.

"Yes, and I think she was trying to keep it a secret," she answered excitedly, clearly unencumbered by worries about disrespecting the dead now.

"Was it someone from in town?"

Shelley grinned and shook her head. "I don't know. She never introduced him to me, but there was someone who had begun visiting her about a month ago. The whole thing had a very secret rendezvous feel to it, though."

My mind raced with ideas about this secret man. Whoever he was, Geneva had succeeded in keeping the relationship completely hidden. None of the usual gossip about her had included any mention of a new man in her life. And whoever this man was, he certainly would be of interest to Derek in trying to figure out who strangled Geneva.

"Can you describe him, Shelley?"

She shook her head again. "Not really. I only saw him a few times, but each time was around midnight or one in the morning. I happened to be looking out my bedroom window Sunday night and saw someone walking through her backyard. It was so dark, though, that I couldn't make out his face."

"That's okay. Even if you can remember how tall he was or if there was anything special you noticed about him any of the times you saw him, it can help."

Closing her eyes, Shelley appeared to be thinking for

a few moments, and then her eyes flew open. "I remember one time in particular because it was the first time he hadn't waited for her to let him in. He walked across the yard and right up onto her back porch and just walked in. Oh, I wish it had been a full moon out that night! Then I would have been able to see more of him. As it was, I only saw he had dark hair and was tall."

"Okay, tall. That's good. And dark hair. Good. Do you remember anything else? Did you hear his voice? Did he say anything any of the times you saw him?"

"No. I'm sorry. My window was closed, so I didn't hear a thing. Do you think this man could have been the one who did it?"

"I don't know," I admitted, trying to remain calm while inside I was dying to get back to the police station to tell Derek about Geneva's mystery man.

"I wish I could help more. Poor Geneva deserves that, at least."

Standing, she bent over and plucked out the pink foam spacers from between her toes, signaling our visit had ended. I followed her to the front door and handed her my business card from the newspaper. "If you think of anything else you'd like to tell me, call me."

Shelley looked down at the card that said "Features Writer" and then her gaze met mine. With a lilt in her voice that seemed odd, she asked, "None of what we said will be in printed in *The Eagle*, will it? I'd hate to see poor Geneva's name dragged through the mud. Someone like her deserves better than that."

I had a feeling she wouldn't have any problem with seeing Geneva's name dragged through anything. A hint of glee seemed to dance in her eyes now.

"I promise you, Shelley, that anything you tell me

will remain confidential. My card is from my job, but I'm here as a good citizen just trying to help find out who did this to her."

We said our goodbyes and then I turned to leave, but Shelley's hand on my arm stopped me. I looked back at her and saw she had more to say.

"I remembered something else about the man I saw. There was something silver that flashed in the light. I don't know what it was, but I remember a tiny gleam of silver when he stepped onto the back porch. Maybe it a ring?"

"Silver? Okay. I'll keep that in mind. Thank you again, Shelley. Stay safe."

She gave me a big smile like she had when I first arrived and as she closed the door, she said, "I'm not worried. Sunset Ridge is a very safe place."

As I walked down the front steps out to the sidewalk on the street, I couldn't help but think she had a misguided feeling of security. For someone whose nearest neighbor had just been murdered, she seemed strangely unfazed.

DEREK STOOD IN his office with a man I'd never seen before. Taller than Derek with dark brown hair and a serious look that screamed authority, he'd positioned himself between the policeman and the door. I stood watching them for a moment trying to ascertain what the meeting was about. Clearly, he wasn't a suspect in any crime. The mystery man didn't appear concerned about what Derek thought about him, and in fact, as I watched them interact, I saw Derek display a level of deference I'd only seen from him toward his older brother.

They turned to face me as I studied them, and for a moment, I felt like an intruder on something private. Stepping back out of the doorway, I mumbled a weak apology.

"Poppy, this is Alexander Montero. Alexander, this is Poppy McGuire."

The man gave me a faint smile and shook my hand when I extended mine. "Nice to meet you."

"Alexander is a retired Baltimore police detective. He lives right here in Sunset Ridge now," Derek explained.

I stood struck by how young this man looked to be retired from anything. He couldn't have been more than a few years older than I, and although he had what appeared like a tiny scar on his cheek, he looked like he could be a model more than a detective. His dark hair was slightly longer than I preferred on men and touched the collar of his white dress shirt, and I saw his body was definitely in great shape, even hidden beneath his clothes.

But what struck me were his deep brown eyes and how full of sadness they looked. Had he been the victim of some crime here in town? Was he related to the Geneva Woodward case?

"It's very nice to meet you, Alexander. Have you lived in Sunset Ridge long?"

"Not long."

Surprised by how terse his response was, I felt compelled to ask another question. "Do you live with your family here in town?"

Alexander narrowed his eyes and for a moment I wasn't sure he'd even answer that one. When he did, it was another abrupt response. "Outside of town."

Derek stood there watching what had turned into a very awkward moment between us, but I couldn't help myself. I had to ask one more question, if only to make myself feel like I'd made a true effort with this new person. "Retirement sounds delightful. Are you enjoying it?"

As he turned to face Derek, he mumbled, "Not really." And then with a quick handshake to the policeman next to him, he left.

Just like that. No goodbye. No nice to meet you. Nothing but a few curt answers to my perfectly polite questions.

I turned around to watch him as he walked out of the police station and then turned back to look at Derek for some explanation for what had just happened. Alexander Montero wasn't going to enjoy his time in Sunset Ridge if he continued to act like that.

"He was so unfriendly! What was that all about?"

Derek sat down behind his desk and nodded his agreement that Alexander had been rude. "I don't know. He's usually a nice guy."

"So it wasn't all in my head? Did I say something wrong?" I asked, suddenly wondering if I'd done something to offend him.

"I wouldn't worry about it. I'm sure the next time you two meet it will be friendlier. I imagined you two would get along famously, to be honest. He was one of the best detectives Baltimore had ever seen. The guy has a sixth sense when it comes to solving crimes."

I wasn't sure I wanted there to be a next time with Alexander Montero if there was a chance he'd be that icy again. It was a shame, too. If he was as terrific a detective as Derek believed, he'd be an interesting person to talk to. In addition, Sunset Ridge had a dearth of attractive, single men, and by the look of that empty ring finger on his left hand, he was definitely unmarried.

"So other than making a bad first impression with him, what brings you back to my office once again today, Poppy? Find out anything interesting in your investigation so far?"

I screwed my expression into a mock grimace at his teasing. "I'll have you know I've found a few things out, Derek. How have you done in my absence?"

Putting his hands behind his head, Derek leaned back in his chair and smiled. "You first. I just hope you haven't been listening to the gossip our fellow Sunset Ridge citizens have been spreading about Geneva. I went to The Grounds for a coffee and heard theories that involved both the CIA and a long lost relative come out of hiding to take all her money. Crazy."

"No, Derek. I've been talking to her next door neighbor, Shelley Steadman. She has some interesting things to say about poor Geneva."

I had to chuckle at my use of the same word to describe her as Shelley had used. Derek didn't pick up on the inside joke and stared at me, waiting to hear what I had to report.

"Shelley claims to have been close friends with Geneva, but my gut says the feeling wasn't mutual. My guess is what made Geneva so standoffish to the rest of town—her way of looking down her nose at anyone who didn't have as much money as she had—rang true in her relationship with Shelley too. She and her new money just didn't realize she was being judged inferior."

Looking unimpressed, Derek shrugged. "So? Geneva

was a snob even to someone who liked her. This doesn't really surprise me, and I don't think it helps with figuring out who murdered her."

I leaned forward toward his desk and grinned at what I had to say next. There was no way Derek would dismiss the information about Geneva's mystery man so easily.

"What if I told you our victim was seeing a man in secret and he only visited her under cover of darkness in the middle of the night?"

Without missing a beat, he answered, "I'd say I find that interesting but not as interesting as what the state police had to report an hour ago."

My thunder stolen, I sat back in my chair. "What did they say?"

Now it was Derek's turn to strike the pose of the victor. Lifting his chin, he grinned and said, "That they caught a thief trying to sell some fine jewelry early this morning. I'm guessing that when we get the inventory of Geneva's things from her insurance company that we're going to find there are some pieces missing. The very pieces the thief was trying to get rid of just a few hours ago."

I shook my head, not believing Derek's all-too-convenient solution to who strangled Geneva. "I don't think so. My gut tells me there's more to this than some guy trying to rob her house and ending up murdering her."

"I'm sorry, Poppy. I know you were looking forward to investigating this, but I think this is going to turn out just as I said earlier—a robbery gone bad. I think our guy was just in the right place at the wrong time and got caught, so he had to kill her. He probably took those rings you were so curious about too."

I stood to leave, undeterred in my conviction that there was far more to this case than a bad coincidence that had led to a woman being strangled. "If you don't mind, I'm going to continue asking questions, even though you're convinced this is all but a closed case."

"As long as you don't get yourself in trouble, feel free. But I think you're on a wild goose chase."

"Well, I don't mind if you don't. I'll let you know what I find out."

Derek nodded, but it was clear he didn't expect me to find out anything that would solve this case. He simply couldn't or wouldn't see that the way she was murdered was too personal for just some stranger to kill her in that way.

But I did. And I intended to prove it.

Chapter Three

I TOOK ADVANTAGE of a beautiful spring day and walked the long way back to my house, my mind running through what Derek had said in an attempt to figure out if I was, in fact, wasting my time on a wild goose chase. The unseasonably warm April weather made me wish I had stashed my running shoes in my bag so I could go for a run and clear my head, but it was better I got home anyway since I had work to do for my job at The Bottom Line.

Researching mundane facts to support a story of a Pennsylvania politician rumored to be stepping out with some young thing would give me a chance to focus on what paid my bills for a while before I turned back to poking around town on Geneva Woodward's case. Whenever I found myself distracted, work always helped to get my mind back on track.

Ten minutes later, I was seated at my desk in the spare bedroom next to my own with a big glass of sweet tea and ready to go. The assignment in Pennsylvania involved a relatively unknown state senator who had been seen coming out of a hotel with a woman who looked nothing like his wife of fifteen years. The Bottom Line had gotten word of his behavior from one of the site's informants who loved to out people like him, and I was given the task of researching all the details to ensure when the story broke there were no inaccuracies.

That's how things worked with my online job. The site acted like an online watercooler where the deepest and darkest secrets of important and quasi-important people were exposed with more glee than I'd ever felt over others' personal lives. It wasn't a terrific job by any means, but it was a job.

As I examined the information about this current philanderer trying to have his cake and eat it too, I thought about my mother and how much I wished she was still with me. Always so supportive of everything I did, she probably wouldn't think too highly of this job and would likely remind me that she'd always hoped I'd become a lawyer or something more honorable. She'd also be the first one to ask why I bothered working at The Bottom Line since she'd left me more than enough to live on without having to help dig up dirt on famous and not-so-famous people.

My mind didn't gain the focus it usually did from work, and I found myself drifting off to think about Geneva Woodward after about an hour. The more I thought about it, the more I was sure the way she was killed showed the relationship of her murderer to her. An impersonal killing involved a gun that could kill someone from a distance. Standing behind someone pulling a scarf tightly around their neck was a sign of some link between murderer and victim.

Some guy stealing her jewelry when she stumbled upon him and couldn't get away fast enough didn't make any sense. A beating death, while up close like strangulation, didn't have the same intimacy. If she came upon some stranger robbing her house and he caught her before she escaped, he might hit her to knock her out so he could run, but taking the time to remove her scarf and then choke her with it?

That said a bond between Geneva and her killer.

And Derek's idea of some guy taking her jewelry didn't fit with the fact that there was no evidence that anyone had forced their way into her house. No, she let the person who killed her in because she knew him. Or her.

I had to admit that I'd been thinking the murderer was a man, even before Shelley told me about her secret nighttime visitor. I knew I should wait until the evidence showed that, but something about strangulation felt masculine.

Not that a woman couldn't have done it. Shelley Steadman hadn't exactly acted like the bereaved best friend she saw herself as when I spoke to her. No matter how many times she referred to her next door neighbor as poor Geneva, the look on her face said that the loss wasn't really breaking her heart.

So if they weren't best friends, what was the relationship between Geneva Woodward and Shelley Steadman? Had it been an awkwardly cool politeness on Geneva's end that Shelley intentionally or unintentionally misinterpreted because she wanted to hang around with someone of Geneva's level?

Or had they truly been friends and equals in both women's eyes and Shelley was just dealing with her neighbor's death in her own slightly unfeeling way?

My head squarely stuck in the case, I put away my work for the time being and let my mind roam to what my next step should be. In the house to the right of

Geneva's lived a young woman and her grandmother, so I needed to talk to both of them. Maybe they too saw this mystery man like Shelley had.

That Shelley had lied had occurred to me, and as I let my mind wander over the details of the case so far, she became my first suspect in the murder of Geneva Woodward. Something about the way she just didn't seem unhappy about her death set off bells for me. True, it was possible she was just a callous person and she'd react to anyone's death in her self-centered way, but it was also possible she had a good reason to be happy Geneva was dead.

And it was just as possible she'd been the one to make her that way.

She was close to Geneva, or at least she claimed to be, so she had opportunity since a friend would let another friend into her house willingly. But could she strangle her? I thought back to my time with Shelley and tried to imagine her positioned behind Geneva. Standing at least three or four inches taller than I did at five foot six, Shelley was definitely taller than her friend, who was about my height. She was also bigger than Geneva, who could best be described as thin. Shelley had the appearance of someone who enjoyed too much of her newfound wealth. Like all that shopping and indulging had given her a soft, meaty look.

I couldn't help but think she had the size and strength necessary to overpower Geneva and strangle her to death. But then there was always the mystery man who visited in the dark of night.

Who was he?

That Geneva could conduct a secret love affair in Sunset Ridge impressed me. As small towns went, it was typical in that everyone seemed to know what everyone else was up to, no matter how much a person tried to keep their goings-on private. I knew firsthand how quickly gossip spread in my hometown, and if someone had gotten a hold of a piece of juicy news like Geneva Woodward having a secret love affair, it would have spread like wildfire.

Closing my eyes, I remembered having to explain to my father the time I began dating Jason Durrow, sneaking out in the middle of the night to go to a party with him and thinking I'd gotten it past my parents, only to find out that the local rumor mill had informed them of everything I'd done just a day later in vivid detail. In a small town, having a private life was next to impossible.

Prying eyes were always on her simply because she was like Sunset Ridge royalty. So how had Geneva kept this man visiting her a secret?

My eyes flew open. She hadn't. Shelley had known. But was it believable that she wouldn't share that piece of gossip? And was it believable that no one else had found out about this mystery man?

I needed to find someone else who saw the overnight comings and goings at Geneva's house. As I set my sights on heading over to Geneva's other next door neighbor, my phone rang and I looked down at the screen to see it was Bethany.

"Hey, what's up?" she asked in response to my hello.

"Just doing some work." That wasn't a complete lie. I had done some work earlier.

"Work work, or trying to figure out who killed Geneva Woodward work?"

I chuckled at how well Bethany knew me. "Well, I tried to get some work done for The Bottom Line, and I guess you could say I succeeded, but I couldn't help it. My brain is stuck on this murder case."

"I still can't believe we have a murderer in town, Poppy. I just got back from a walk to the bank, and all I could think was that I might have passed him or her on the street. They might have been right next to me, and I wouldn't even have known it."

Bethany's assessment was right on the nose. The murderer was very likely someone from town who we both had seen hundreds of times. "I know. I can't help thinking that too. It's not like we get that many newcomers here. I mean, the Hotel Piermont is rarely more than half full on any given night."

"And that's more like a bed and breakfast anyway, so it isn't like half full means hundreds of people arriving in town," Bethany added.

"Well, only if bed and breakfasts had a seedy feel to them," I joked. "And we all know that the most common type of person that hotel gets is the husband who's been thrown out of his house by an angry wife."

Bethany giggled as she described the other main types of visitors the Hotel Piermont got. "Don't forget the couples who go there for a quickie and cheaters."

I tried to imagine Geneva being involved in anything called a quickie. No way. I didn't know what she was up to, but I couldn't see her checking into the local hotel for some afternoon delight. Plus, if what Shelley had said was true, Geneva was using her own home for her trysts.

Knowing I shouldn't tell Bethany about that detail, I changed the subject to my unpleasant first meeting with Alexander Montero. "While I was at Derek's office at the station today, I met someone new."

As few new people ever came to town, she reacted

with surprise. "Someone new in Sunset Ridge? Had he been arrested?"

"No. He seemed to be someone Derek knew. His name is Alexander and he was a Baltimore policeman. Well, he was before he retired."

Bethany's disappointment came out in a deep sigh. "Just what we need. Some fat, old retired cop. I bet he's bald, isn't he? Why don't we ever get hot guys coming to this town? Just once I'd like to hear one of us say that we met a hot guy and he's single. Is that too much to ask?"

I thought about Alexander and smiled. "Your wish seems to have come true. He's retired, but I don't think he could be any older than thirty-five, if that. And he's good looking. I mean very good looking."

"Are you kidding? How is it I haven't seen him yet? I'm out every day in this town, and I haven't seen this mythical creature you speak of roaming the streets of Sunset Ridge."

"And although I don't know for sure, I think he's single."

My bombshell made Bethany go silent for a moment, but when she'd recovered, she said, "I hear something strange in your voice, Poppy. You say he's very good looking and single, yet you don't sound like you're that impressed. What's up?"

The memory of Alexander's rude behavior floated through my mind, and I grimaced. No matter how good looking he was, acting that way was never okay.

"Let's just say he didn't make me want to run off with him to the Hotel Piermont this afternoon. He has the personality of a piranha."

"What do you mean?" she asked, no doubt curious about him since I rarely said anything that negative about people.

"He was really quite rude, to be honest. I asked a few polite questions just to break the ice, and he barely could mutter one word answers. As far as I'm concerned, it doesn't matter how gorgeous a man is. If he can't be bothered to even be pleasant when he meets someone for the first time, then I can't be bothered to give him the time of day."

"So he was gorgeous, huh?"

Bethany had a terrible way of focusing on all the wrong things. Her history with men wasn't exactly stellar, and it was littered with more failures than successes, mainly because she went after all the wrong men.

"Looks aren't everything," I said, chastising her. "A gorgeous face and body fade over time and then what are you left with? Some surly guy who's rude."

"So he was gorgeous and had a great body?" she asked excitedly.

I stood from my desk to stretch my legs after hours of sitting and took a deep breath. "You're just going to ignore what I said about his piranha personality, aren't you?"

"No. Well, maybe. It's just that with so few good looking men around, a girl can't be too choosy, Poppy. I keep telling you that."

"And I keep ignoring you. I think I need to make myself something to eat. I've been at my desk for hours, so it's time for a snack break. I'll talk to you tomorrow, okay?"

"Okay. I'm going back to my boring job to fantasize about this new guy in town. Thanks for giving me something to pass the rest of the day away."

I rolled my eyes at her silliness about men. "You're too funny. Talk to you later."

After a snack of some crackers with cheese and more iced tea, I thought about walking over to talk to Geneva's other next door neighbors but I couldn't get Alexander Montero out of my mind. Unlike Bethany, I had no problem not wanting men who were bad for me. Bad boys, by their very nature, weren't good for me, but I didn't have the sense that Alexander was bad.

In fact, he seemed more angry than bad. That difference made me curious about him. If he'd been simply bad, I wouldn't have given him another thought, but angry people were hiding something.

So what was Alexander Montero hiding?

The internet is a wonderful thing for finding out the answer to that very question. And I was no regular online stalker. Nope, this girl knew how to search in ways most other people had no idea of. If there was something in his background and history, I'd find it.

I decided to start with the obvious. If he'd been a Baltimore police detective, then there would be newspaper articles that mentioned him. That was my first stop to find out what Alexander Montero was hiding.

Sometimes a search yielded a paltry few results at first, and yet other times all I had to do was type in a name and a person's entire life came up on the screen in front of me. However, Alexander's name made neither of these things happen. I certainly found a plethora of articles containing his name, and they all pointed to the same conclusion.

He'd been one hell of an investigator when he was a cop. Of course, that begged the question as to why he'd left that job. Even assuming he'd become an officer in his early to mid-twenties, retiring less than a decade later seemed strange for someone who'd been as successful as he'd been. He'd risen to the rank of detective in record time, according to one write-up about him.

So why did he retire so young?

I searched for any information that might indicate he'd been hurt on the job and found it less than fifteen minutes later. He'd suffered an injury from a shooting on the job in 2010, but it hadn't been life threatening. The wound had earned him a commendation from the mayor himself, and it appeared he returned to work in a little over a month.

But he didn't retire right after that. Had the shooting made him leave the job, or was it something else?

For over two hours, I searched through everything I could find on Alexander Montero. Much of it involved his job, but one search result came up not with his name but with the name Helena Montero. An obituary, it listed her as passing away five years ago at the age of twenty-eight. As I read through the last things written about her life, I saw her husband had been named Alexander. The write-up mentioned no children but told of how she'd been a chef at a well-known Baltimore restaurant and a kind person who helped out those in need whenever she could.

Reading about her made me feel bad about looking up information on Alexander, and I closed my laptop without searching any further. I'd found what I was looking for. He was exactly what Derek had said he was.

A great detective who had retired early.

But I couldn't help but wonder if that woman named Helena had been his wife. What happened to her to make her die so young? And was her death why Alexander had left the force and moved to Sunset Ridge?

Was that why he seemed so angry?

Chapter Four

MCGUIRE'S BAR HAD been a part of Sunset Ridge since before I was born. My father loved to tell the story of how he came to own the bar that used to be called The Watering Hole. One night he was playing poker with the owner of the bar, a notorious womanizer and gambler named Campbell Grave, and in one hand the man lost his business to my father. I was sure with each retelling that my father left out some of the more important parts of the story, but I never asked mostly because I didn't want to think badly of my father and something told me he hadn't gotten the bar entirely legally. Nevertheless, from that night, he'd owned the bar and Campbell hadn't been seen in Sunset Ridge.

I took a seat at the bar and hung my purse from the hook near my knees as my father poured me a glass of my favorite beer, a summer wheat he'd arranged to keep stocked up on year round so I could have it any time I wanted. That's the kind of man my father was.

Taking a sip, I let the taste of it linger on my tongue before I swallowed. No matter if it was freezing cold outside or on the cusp of warmer weather like it was earlier that day, drinking this particular beer made me think of sultry summer nights on my back porch having a good time with friends.

"So what's new with my Poppy?" he asked with one of his trademark big Irish grins.

I thought about my day and tried to find a way to explain it. A murder in Sunset Ridge. Taking on my first criminal investigation. Some work done at both my jobs. And meeting someone who seemed to take an instant dislike to me. It had been a full day.

Finally, after deciding there was no great way to describe it, I answered, "A lot. Not much. It's hard to explain."

"You look like you have a lot on your mind, honey. Something bothering you?"

I hesitated to tell my father about Derek's allowing me to poke around asking questions about his case. My father had a tendency to worry about me, and hearing I was involved in a murder investigation likely wouldn't give him much peace of mind.

He'd find out anyway, though, so I just had to find the right words to break the news. As any daughter knew, it wasn't what to say but how to say it that mattered.

"I'm fine, Dad. I took on a new job today. Well, it's sort of a job, and my mind's been busy mulling it over all day."

My father wiped down the bar in front of him with a damp cloth and nodded. "Sounds good. Anything you want to talk about?"

"I'm helping Derek, sort of, with one of his cases. Nothing big. Just working some things out for him."

My attempt at finding the right words was failing spectacularly if the confused look on my father's face was any indication. Well, when in doubt, I'd always found being truthful was the only way to go. Taking a deep breath in, I exhaled slowly and then did just that.

"I'm helping Derek with the Geneva Woodward murder case."

I waited for my father to begin lecturing me on the danger of a murder investigation and how I wasn't part of the police, but it never came. Instead, he smiled and slowly nodded, as if he was processing what I'd said and weighing his response. When he finally spoke, his voice was surprisingly even.

"I could ask how this happened or tell you I'm going to be worried sick about you doing this, but there really isn't a point, is there? You're just like your mother. Always so curious. I just want to know you're going to be careful. Someone murdered Geneva, Poppy, and that person is going to do anything to keep from being found out. I need you to tell me you know that."

Reaching across the bar, I took his hands in mine and looked him dead in the eye. "I know that, Dad, and I'm going to be careful. I promise. Thank you for understanding and being supportive of me in this."

He squeezed my hands and with a chuckle said, "I wouldn't call what I'm feeling support, sweetheart. I do understand, though. As I said, you're so much like your mother. She never could let a mystery go, no matter what it meant. Her patients loved her for it, though."

The sadness in his voice when he talked about my mother still lingered, even after her death nearly a decade ago. I knew how he felt. I missed her too. Sometimes the loss pressed so heavy on my heart I couldn't imagine how I'd get through to tomorrow.

I hated seeing him like that, so I quickly moved to change the subject. "So what do you think of this

Geneva Woodward murder case, Dad? Derek says it's been years since a murder was committed in Sunset Ridge."

My father nodded. "He's right. It's been a very long time since the police had to solve that kind of crime. I'm sure Derek's feeling like fish out of water right about now."

"Well, I'm helping, and anyway, he doesn't even think it was a murder so much as a robbery gone bad. I think he's crazy."

"Geneva Woodward. Now there's a story," he said as he folded his arms across his chest. "Small town royalty is what they used to call the Woodwards."

"They still do. She certainly acted like she was head and shoulders above the rest of us," I said as I took a drink of my beer, instantly thinking I'd been disrespectful of the dead. "That wasn't nice. I'm sorry."

"Don't be. That woman was a piece of work."

My father's snide remark about Geneva surprised me. I leaned back away from the bar and chuckled. "Is there something you'd like to share, Dad? It sounds like you knew her better than I did."

"You could say that."

His coyness made me want to know what he had to say even more. "Well, are you going to give me the details? I've never heard you talk about her at all, so this makes me curious. What are you hiding?"

"I'm not hiding anything," he said as he rolled his eyes. "I just happened to see her more than you did. She used to come in right before closing time when everyone was already gone for the night."

"Are you saying Geneva had the hots for my father?"

He shrugged and said, "The hots for me? Well, I guess."

The thought of her wanting any man surprised me, strangely enough, even though Shelley had said there was a mystery man in her life. She was so cold and imperial in her ways whenever I saw her in town that thinking of her as a sensual being just didn't work.

"Are you going to give me the details, or do I have to beg?"

My father poured himself a glass of soda and slowly took a drink. He liked to play games like this because he knew I could be impatient. When he finally answered, it was more non-answers, in truth.

"She and I never went out, if that's what you're asking. I wasn't interested, but I can say she was insistent. She'd come in every night a few minutes before two and sit down right where you're sitting. I can't say she ever propositioned me directly, but she made it clear that she was interested in knowing more about me."

"How long did this go on?"

Looking up toward the ceiling, he thought about my question and sighed as he lowered his head. "I want to say about three weeks. She just stopped one night about a month ago. Not that I wasn't relieved."

"Geneva Woodward could have been my stepmother. Wow! I'd never think that was possible in a million years," I teased.

Turning serious, he frowned and shook his head. "It wasn't possible. Isn't possible. There is no other woman for me but your mother."

His words pinched at my heart, and for a long moment I remained silent. I knew my father meant what he said. He'd never remarry again, so he'd be alone for the rest of his life because he still loved my mother and he'd never hurt another woman like that. He was an honest man, and even though I wished more than he knew that he'd let himself love again, he wouldn't.

It just wasn't who he was. He'd found the love of his life, and he didn't want to move on.

"So she chased you for three weeks and then gave up when she found out she couldn't get you. Interesting."

"I don't know if it's that interesting, Poppy. I think she might have been a lonely woman in her forties who just wanted some company. No crime in that."

I took a drink of my beer and thought about the crime that had occurred. Geneva had been after my father until someone else came along. Maybe my father had seen her mystery lover around her one of those nights.

"Dad, was Geneva always alone with you? There was never anyone else here when she came in to see you every night?"

"No, just the two of us. Well, no that's not true. Once or twice there were other people here. I think Candy Skerritt was still in the bar one time, and the usual characters were here too."

Tipping my glass up, I drank the last of my beer and handed my father the empty glass. "Thanks for the drink, Dad. I better head home. I've got an early day at *The Eagle* tomorrow."

"Anytime, honey. I want you to promise me again that you're going to stay safe while you do this with Derek."

I spun around on my barstool and stood to leave, just like I used to do when I was a little girl and it was time for me to go because my father had to open the bar. He came toward me to give me a hug and squeezed me tightly to him.

The feel of his arms holding me always made me feel safe and secure. Ever since I was young, just a hug from my father let me know I everything would be all right. I may have been all grown up and out on my own, but his expression of how much he loved me never failed to bring a smile to my face.

"I promise, Dad. I'll be fine. You know me."

He leaned back away from me and gave me a skeptical look. "That's supposed to make me feel good about this?"

True, I did have a long history of getting into trouble. Well, scrapes would be a better description of what usually happened. But I never really got hurt, so he had nothing to worry about.

I cradled his face in my palms and smiled up at him. "You worry too much, Dad. Remember, this is Sunset Ridge."

"Where one of the most important people in town has just been murdered."

He never missed a beat.

"Well, then feel better because your daughter is smart and she's going to solve this case."

He kissed me on the tip of my nose and sighed. "Just like your mother. Don't forget not everyone is as kind and good as you are, Elizabeth. There are bad people in this world, and at least one of them killed Geneva and likely may still be here in town. This isn't some tawdry gossip story you're used to working on. Whoever killed Geneva isn't above hurting someone like you. Remember that."

"I will, Dad. I'm a big girl now. I can take care of

myself."

The look on his face told me he didn't believe that last part. Kissing him goodnight, I left the bar and headed home as night began to fall. The news that Geneva Woodward had been interested in my father still rambled around my brain, but even more intriguing was the idea that around the same time she was pursuing my father, if Shelley was right, there was another man who was pursuing her.

Had he been the one to take her life?

BY ELEVEN THE next morning, I was behind my desk at *The Sunset Ridge Eagle* after a night of tossing and turning what I knew about Geneva Woodward over in my mind at least a hundred times. My father's news had made me rethink the kind of person she'd been. If she had taken an interest in my father, then maybe she wasn't all stone and ice behind that snobbish façade she presented to everyone.

But my job as the social events writer for the town's newspaper called, and even though I was eager to investigate the case further, my responsibilities trumped my curiosity. So the mystery of who killed Geneva had to wait a few hours while I did my part in the rat race.

My assignment this week focused on the Founders' Day Festival that would take center stage in town in June. A yearly celebration of all things Sunset Ridge had to offer, the newspaper planned to focus on the town's humble beginnings as a stopover point for troops between Baltimore and Philadelphia in the Revolutionary War period, its modern day claim at being the perfect town close to major cities and fresh country air while offering a safe, suburban environment for everyone, and everything in between.

My editor had stressed repeatedly how important this series of articles would be to the town, but I had to wonder how the claim to being a safe place to live would stand up under the reality that a murder had been committed and the victim was one of Sunset Ridge's most prominent citizens.

I hadn't heard from Howard yet about any of these issues, so either he was in complete denial or didn't know. The latter reason was just as likely as the former since he'd become a new father three months ago. It had made him a slightly happier person, but his work had definitely suffered from this newfound joy at home.

Not that Geneva's death would change anything about the Founders' Day celebration necessarily. The main focus of the event was always the great history of the area, and it would be that again this year. The planning committee, which doubled as the self-appointed town decorating committee for major holidays, would see to that.

Comprised of four women, the Founders' Day Planning Committee, as they demanded they be called, oversaw every moment of the upcoming event. From what buildings in town would be decorated to the order of the procession in the big parade, the four ladies on the committee ruled with an iron hand. Each year they dealt with any number of residents who wanted to introduce something new into the event or change the parade route to help their business, and always the answer from the women was the same.

Delivered in a handwritten note, each dissenter was told, "No. We have always done it this way, and we will continue to do it this way."

It was this group of women I had to meet to write my series of articles. Although I knew each of them separately and had spoken to a couple of them in the past for write-ups on Founders' Day, this would be the first time I had the opportunity to speak to the formal committee.

I wasn't looking forward to it.

Mrs. Joseph Scanlon, whose first name I had never learned even though I'd known her since I was a little girl, was the unofficial chairwoman of the planning committee. Married to James Scanlon for nearly forty years, she was almost sixty and looked like she'd slaved away for every day of those years, despite the fact that she hadn't worked since sometime during the Carter administration. Her eyes had been grey for as long as anyone had known her, but now they matched her steel grey hair, an aged version of the long brown hair she'd had as a young woman.

She knew my mother and often came by our house when I was a child. I remembered each time she visited she'd bring brightly colored cookies she made especially for me that looked like fruit but always tasted more like chemicals. And every time she made a point of telling me how much care she'd taken to make them just right. By the time I was a teenager, I was convinced she was trying to kill me.

Only one of her fellow committee members, the Widow Dunn, acted older than Mrs. Scanlon. That she insisted on being called by such an archaic title baffled me, but that's the way she required the world to address her.

The Widow Dunn. She sounded like some dreadful

character from a horror film involving missing children.

Her actual name was Arlene Dunn, which sounded far less frightening and didn't make me feel like I'd taken a trip back to the eighteenth century every time I had to address her. In her late forties, she looked far younger than the committee's chairwoman and loved to brag about how nature had taken so much from her but had left her with a beautifully smooth face untouched by wrinkles and lustrous black hair without a single grey strand to be found in it.

Everyone in town knew she dyed her hair. It was impossible to not know. The shade of black she used had never occurred in nature, other than in permanent markers, and the color made her resemble an older version of Snow White more than anything else. Her vanity knew no bounds, though, so no one had bothered to say anything to her about her boast in years, even though she continued to make it any time she had the chance.

Her husband, Andrew Dunn, had been one of the wealthiest men in Sunset Ridge and twenty years older than her when they married. After less than ten years of wedded bliss together, he passed away at the age of fifty-one, leaving her a widow of barely thirty with his fortune and three sons under the age of ten to raise. Since then, she'd demanded everyone in town call her the Widow Dunn as she waved her wealth around to get her way, no matter who was put out.

Joining them was my former English teacher from junior year at Sunset Ridge High School, Eileen Matthews. The youngest member of the committee and not even forty yet, she was consistently overruled by the other women every time she wanted to inject some new idea into the celebration. A replacement for her mother Evelyn, who had been forced to step down from the committee three years ago after having a stroke, Eileen Matthews seemed an unlikely addition to the group, but she stayed, nonetheless, even though she had little effect.

Unmarried, she was devoted to her career teaching teenagers the proper way to read American literature. She'd taught my favorite class of all four years in high school, and while I enjoyed seeing her when we met on the street from time to time, she seemed a little less chipper and bright since her mother's illness.

And finally there was Mrs. Eleanor Girard, the First Lady of Sunset Ridge. Technically, the former first lady because her husband wasn't the mayor anymore since last year's election that sent him out of office after twelve years, she refused to relinquish the title now correctly held by the current mayor's wife, Christine Sanders. She'd been told by a number of very prominent people in town that it was inappropriate to continue calling herself the First Lady, but that hadn't changed her mind.

If anything, it had made her more insistent on keeping the title. She'd walk up and down Main Street with her flash of red hair falling onto her face as she waved to people and waited for everyone to address her as First Lady. So that's what people called her. Most understood that she had never accomplished anything on her own, so letting her run around town calling herself that did few people harm, even if it did make her look foolish. In Sunset Ridge, it was a matter of respect mixed with a heady dose of letting someone keep their illusions because if she didn't, she'd have little more than a sham marriage and a nice house to lay claim to.

These were the people I had to spend my time with

to write my article and make my editor happy. After three missed meetings because of one or another issues the ladies had come up, today was the day the five of us would meet. The Widow Dunn insisted the meeting take place at her house since it was, as she had bluntly said to me on the phone, "the finest of the four homes it could be held at."

Her need to put on airs seemed unnecessary since their usual place for the bi-monthly meetings of the decorating committee was the back room of my father's bar, but I assumed she wanted to show off some new piece of artwork or another set of expensive china to make her fellow committee members jealous. So off to the Widow Dunn's house I went to be on time for my one o'clock meeting.

If I was lucky, they'd have something to say about the murder victim that could help me figure out what had happened to take Geneva from this earth. If I was really lucky, they'd be their usual nosy selves and point me right toward the killer.

Chapter Five

A S I APPROACHED the Dunn house, I saw it was located only one block away from Geneva's house. Perhaps the widow would know something about who may have been visiting her before her death. Climbing the stairs to the wide porch on the front of the large older home, I promised myself if I could, I'd direct the conversation to the story everyone in town was talking about and see if I could learn something more about Geneva's nighttime visits.

Eileen Matthews met me at the door and walked with me toward the very opulent sitting room where the meeting was to be held. As we made our way there, she talked about the weather and how her students were doing, but I had a sense she wanted to talk about something else. Just before we reached the room, she gently grabbed my wrist and stopped me.

"The women are in rare form today, Poppy. I won't be surprised if you get very little out of them for your article. But if you need more information after today, feel free to call me."

I looked at her, surprised at what she'd said, and asked, "Is there something wrong with the committee members?"

She shook her head and smiled. "No. I just don't think with what's going on in town lately that you're going to get much from them but gossip today. I might be wrong. Who knows? Just remember you can get the information from me later, if you need to."

As she walked away to take her seat in Arlene Dunn's sitting room, I hoped I'd hear more about Geneva than the Founders' Day celebration or their plans for every holiday they planned to decorate the streets of town for. Perhaps this wouldn't be as bad as I'd initially thought.

The four women sat in burgundy upholstered chairs set up in a semi-circle and all aimed at a single similar chair I was supposed to sit in. I hadn't taken two steps into the room before the Widow Dunn extended her arm and pointed toward the lone empty seat.

"Sit down, Miss McGuire. It is still miss, isn't it?" she asked in the voice of a police interrogator.

I did as instructed and pressed a smile onto my lips. Still miss. As if being a single woman in her early thirties in the twenty-first century was cause for some kind of gossip. As my cheeks began to ache from forcing my smile, I couldn't help but think if I lived in a bigger city I wouldn't have to field questions like this.

"Yes, it is, ma'am."

"It really is getting down to the wire concerning that, isn't it, dear?" she asked, not even bothering to hide her disgust at my choice of still being unmarried.

The Widow Dunn had apparently decided it was the eleventh hour for this single girl and her chances for happiness. How nice of her.

Quickly changing the topic, I glanced at all four women. "Thank you for taking the time to sit down with me today to talk about the Founders' Day celebration and the wonderful plans you have for decorating our beautiful little town."

Mrs. Scanlon spoke first to begin our meeting, as was customary since she was the chairwoman. Returning my smile, she waved her hand in front of her, as if to dismiss the formal tone of my introduction. "We're all friends here, Poppy. You remember how I used to visit your mother when you were just a little girl? I used to make my fruit cookies especially for you."

"I do. I love thinking back to those days."

And the way your cookies always tasted like you were trying to poison me.

"Your mother would be so proud of you, dear. You were the light of her life."

"Thank you. I appreciate that, Mrs. Scanlon."

"I bet your father is looking forward to some grandchildren, Poppy," the Widow Dunn piped up.

And there it was again. Still miss and no grandchildren for your dear father. Clearly, I was a total failure as a daughter. An unmarried, childless failure.

Taking out my notebook and pen, I crossed my legs and completely ignored Arlene Dunn's jab. "So I know *The Eagle*'s readers are dying to know what wonderful things you ladies have planned for Founders' Day this year."

And that's all it took. One carefully chosen word with the correct emphasis placed on it and they were off to the races.

Wide-eyed and eager, the First Lady jumped on the idea of dying and said, "I can't believe we're going to sit here talking about pie eating contests and balloon colors instead of talking about what's on all of our minds.

Geneva Woodward finally ran into someone who didn't think she was town royalty."

The other three ladies' mouths dropped open as they stared in silence for a long moment at Eleanor Girard after her snipe at the dead woman. Her remark wasn't very politically correct, but that wasn't surprising. I couldn't remember when the First Lady truly acted the part she loved to claim as her own.

Covering her mouth, Mrs. Scanlon erupted into nervous chuckling. "I'm sure Poppy thinks we're just dreadful, but the truth was Geneva wasn't the person she pretended to be."

My ears perked up at this second swipe at poor Geneva. Maybe now we could all get our focus off my still being a single woman and where it should be.

On the dead woman they clearly all wanted to gossip about.

I wasn't sure I should ask any questions regarding Geneva, so I kept my mouth shut and waited in the hopes that the four women in front of me would be exactly what I'd always known them to be.

They didn't disappoint.

"I don't see any point in pretending simply because Miss McGuire is here. I'm sure she knows there was always something phony about Geneva Woodward."

With a simple smile, I let the Widow Dunn know there was no reason for any pretending just because I was there. If they only knew how eager I was to hear what they had to say.

"See that smirk? Our young friend here knows what we're talking about. I mean, can you imagine how many people Geneva offended acting the way she did? Walking around like she was some kind of special princess. I'm surprised she didn't get herself a tiara."

The other three women around her nodded their heads in agreement, and Mrs. Girard continued the character assassination with an attack a little more personal. Smoothing her bright red hair, she tilted her chin up to mimic how Geneva often looked as she appeared in town.

"She had the nerve to actually walk up to me one time right after the election and tell me that it was high time I stopped calling myself First Lady and start acting like the ordinary person I'd always been. The nerve! My husband's tenure as mayor of this town was the most successful in the history of Sunset Ridge, and for someone the likes of her coming from the kind of money her family made their fortune with—"

Eileen Matthews cut her off before the Widow Dunn could jump in and repeat the often whispered bootlegging story that many believed explained how the Woodward family had come into their money. For me, it was the only part of Geneva that had ever seemed interesting, but obviously the women in front of me saw it as some kind of slur.

"Nevermind about that. How about how she had all that money and routinely refused to contribute not one dime to any town functions or events? I must have asked her ten times if I asked her once to give to the school fund, and every time she sneered at me like I was some beggar she couldn't stand to be near. All that money and she was as cheap as they come."

I finally spoke up and said, "I had no idea she was like that, Eileen. I'd always heard she was one of the town's prominent citizens."

The Widow Dunn snorted her derision at my

comment, and Mrs. Scanlon gently tried to bring the conversation back to the day's planned topic. "We have a number of wonderful plans for the Founders' Day event this year, Poppy. The one I'm most excited about is the Miss Little Sunset Ridge beauty pageant. I think it's going to be very special."

I pretended to write down the information about the kiddie beauty competition, but I was more interested in taking notes on all the juicy tidbits the ladies had about Geneva.

"That's very interesting, Mrs. Scanlon. I'm sure it will be a great success," I said with as much enthusiasm as I could fake.

"Yes, yes, Sabrina. That's all well and good, but I know the reason you don't want to talk about Geneva Woodward. If anyone in this town hated her, it was you," the Widow Dunn said with a grin.

The blood drained from Mrs. Scanlon's face, and she turned to face the widow. "Like I was the only one who would have hated her for that reason. And it doesn't matter because it wasn't true. She and Joseph never did that."

I sat in shock at the realization that Mrs. Scanlon had just alluded to her husband cheating on her with Geneva Woodward, so surprised that I didn't even think to jot anything down in my notes.

Arlene Dunn didn't stop her needling, though. Intent on bringing all of Geneva's dirt out into the open, she continued, "I heard otherwise. And I heard that there were quite a few husbands in this town who she'd slept with over the years."

Forgetting my journalistic manners, I let the investigator in me take over and asked, "Who were these men?"

Mrs. Scanlon jumped at the chance to distract everyone from her husband's possible affair with Geneva and offered several names. "Jacob Dernan, Michael Travers, and John Mitchell are the names I've heard. The affairs never lasted very long, though. I think it was just a matter of her retaliating against the wives for some slight she thought they'd made against her. She was that kind of person."

My mind spun and my fingers gripped my pen tightly as I wrote the names of each man and a question mark next to each one. Had Geneva Woodward been the mistress of all these men, or was this just some smear jealous wives used to make themselves feel better about not being at her level?

Mrs. Gerard joined in with her own gossip about the victim. Leaning toward me, she pointed at my notebook and said, "And I know for a fact there were several occasions where the police had to go to her house because there were problems. I bet it was one of the wives who went to confront her. That's what I would have done if I thought she was messing around with my husband. I would have put a stop to that right then and there."

"Do you think one of those women could be the murderer?" Eileen Matthews asked with a look of curiosity in her eyes she directed at me.

I shrugged, not wanting to say much of anything about the case to these women. I preferred to let them chatter away in the hopes that something they said might help me find out who killed Geneva. Thankfully, the Widow Dunn chimed in with her own answer.

"If I were the police and I was looking into it, I'd be

looking at each of those women. If the rumors are correct, and I personally think they were just the tip of the iceberg, then all three of them had a justifiable right to do that. Geneva Woodward liked to act like she was above everyone else in town, but she was just a tramp."

I felt my eyes nearly bug out of my head at Arlene Dunn's calling Geneva a tramp. The ladies around her didn't seem as shocked, though. Even Eileen Matthews, my sweet high school English teacher, nodded in agreement.

What seemed strange was that I'd never heard anything like these accusations against Geneva, even as I'd heard the bootlegging story a number of times over the years.

Curious about that, I asked, "Was this common knowledge? I've never heard of her being anything like this. She seemed to always be alone, as far as I could tell. I mean, she ate dinner by herself at Diamanti's three or four times a week."

"That's what she wanted everyone in town to think, but from what I hear, she was very busy in her private life," Eleanor Girard said smugly. That her husband the former mayor would be the last person on earth anyone would want to have an affair with was all I could think of as I watched her look sideways toward Mrs. Scanlon.

"The First Lady is correct, Poppy. None of us may have ever been present to see the goings on at her home, and we may not have direct knowledge of her activities, but surely we can all agree that behind every bit of gossip is a kernel of truth."

Once again, each of the women around her nodded their heads in agreement, and while I didn't necessarily think she was wrong, I figured I should stay as neutral as possible in case any of them had more information that might be useful. So instead of nodding, I gave her my usual smile that was more polite than committed to anything she'd said.

"I certainly hope this won't affect the festivities in June," I said sweetly, remembering my editor's warning about how important this assignment was not only to the paper but to my job.

"Never," Mrs. Scanlon said confidently. "I won't allow it. Plus, I have no doubt that our fine police will use all their due diligence to solve this case long before Founders' Day. I expect they'll have their murderer shortly."

I was sure my surprise at hearing something complimentary about the Sunset Ridge police was written all over my face. Even my father had expressed doubt that they'd be able to catch the killer.

"That's good to hear. I believe they're hard at work on the case."

Mrs. Scanlon finally corralled the rest of her committee so we could get back to the topic of my series of articles, and in a flash, the discussion changed from Geneva to how wonderful the yearly celebration of the town's history would be this time around.

By nearly four o'clock, I'd gotten all the information I could ever want or need about their plans for Founders' Day, the decorations they planned to add for next year's holiday season, and each of their backgrounds, which they believed I should include in the articles, of course. I'd also gleaned a good amount of information about what they all thought about Geneva Woodward. To say it had been a far more interesting afternoon than I'd anticipated was an understatement.

I hurried over to the police station to see if Derek knew about any of the accusations the committee had made about Geneva's private life. I found him busy with an older man making a complaint about his neighbors parking in front of his house illegally.

This was what being a police officer in Sunset Ridge had consisted of, for the most part, for much of the time Derek had been on the force. His calm way of dealing with the elderly gentleman and giving him something to be happy about as he walked past me on his way out was the real key to Derek's ability. He may not have instilled confidence in many around town, but I had faith he'd do just as Mrs. Scanlon said and would solve Geneva's case.

Just as soon as he saw it for what it was.

"Poppy, you're a sight for sore eyes. Come in and tell me you have something good to give me about the case," he said as he cracked his neck.

I sat down in front of his desk and flipped open my tablet to the notes I'd taken that afternoon. "I had to meet with the ladies of the Founders' Day committee today, and they had some very interesting things to say about poor Geneva."

Derek rolled his eyes. "The committee, huh? Let me guess. They claimed Geneva was sleeping with all the husbands in town, right?"

My shoulders hunched from my disappointment. "I hoped to give you a clue you could work with. You know about the rumors already?"

"Yep. Unless I've missed something lately, I'm guessing they gave you the names Jacob Dernan, John Mitchell, and Michael Travers."

"Yeah, and Joseph Scanlon too, if what the Widow Dunn thinks is correct. Nothing good there?"

Shaking his head, he chuckled. "Nope. I already checked out that old chestnut. I know where each of them and their wives were during the time when the murder would have occurred, and they all have airtight alibis. Anyway, I'm not even sure there's a shred of truth to any of those rumors about Geneva. Did those cranky old ladies give you anything else?"

I scanned my notes and found what Eleanor Girard had mentioned about the police being called to the Woodward house. Maybe that could be something that would help Derek with the case.

"The First Lady claims that there were some kind of issues that required the police to go to Geneva's house. She didn't go into detail about what those problems might have been, though I got the feeling she thought it had something to do with her sex life."

His eyes opened wide in surprise. "Is she saying that someone called the police on Geneva while she was having sex?"

"No, no. I just meant she acted like Geneva was doing something that would get the police called on her. Did you go out on any of those calls?"

He typed something into his computer and ran his finger down the screen. "There's no record of any calls made about Geneva Woodward. Not only that, but according to our records, she never called the police either. We've never been over there."

I sat back in my chair confused. The First Lady had been so sure of that piece of information. "That doesn't make sense. Why would Eleanor Girard say that if it wasn't true?"

"I have no idea, Poppy. This is the same woman who makes everyone still call her the First Lady, as if she was the wife of the damn president at some point. Her husband lost the election, but she still walks around like she's Mrs. Sunset Ridge. I think she might be crazy."

"But it's such an easy thing to check. It seems bizarre that she'd lie about those calls if they never happened."

Derek waved off my concern about Eleanor Girard's claims. "This kind of thing happens all the time in police work, Poppy. It feels like most of the time you're chasing down leads that go nowhere. Thanks for keeping your ears open out there, though."

"No problem. I'm going to head home. It's been a long day of listening to those women. I think I need a drink."

He laughed and nodded. "I have days like that too. Don't get too stressed out about this case, though. Like I said before, I think it's just a robbery gone bad and Geneva Woodward was in the wrong place at the wrong time."

I stood to leave since there was no point discussing that. I didn't believe it any more at that moment than I had the first time he said it. "Have a good night, Derek. I'll be sure to keep you in the loop if I hear anything."

"Thanks, Poppy. Go home and have that drink. My guess is after spending time with those women, you deserve it."

With a wave, I left him as he got ready to go visit the elderly man's neighbors about their illegal parking, but I believed I was onto something with my theory of the case. This was no robbery gone bad but a personal attack on Geneva that ended in her death, intentional or not.

But this being my first case, I needed some help and I couldn't think of anyone better than a former

Baltimore police detective. I just hoped Alexander Montero would be friendlier on our second meeting than he was on our first.

Chapter Six

ALEXANDER'S HOUSE JUST south of town on Miller Road was exactly the kind of place I thought he'd live in. Away from other houses with the closest one half a mile away, it seemed very much secluded and alone.

Just like him.

A large newer house, it made me think of a cabin in the woods the way it was surrounded by large trees. So different from the older, more traditional homes in town, it still looked as impressive as those Victorians.

I pulled up to the front of the house and saw it almost completely dark except for one lone light toward the back. His car sat in the driveway, a sweet looking black '69 Mustang with a hood scoop. Definitely not what I expected him to drive. I hadn't pegged him for a car guy. As the daughter of a man who loved muscle cars, I knew my fair share about them and couldn't help but be impressed by Alexander's choice of wheels. After I admired the car for a few seconds, I turned toward to check out the house, but it looked deserted.

Curious and wanting to get his opinion on the Geneva Woodward murder, I shut off the engine in my Jeep and hopped out. Maybe he was outside chopping wood or doing something out back since it was just after sundown. I walked up to the front door to knock, just in case in he was inside, but as I guessed would happen, I got no answer. So I headed around back in the hope that I'd find him there.

All I found was a newly planted garden, some shrubs that sat waiting to be put into the ground, and a garden shovel. Looking around, I couldn't help but like what I saw, though. The backyard went on for as far as I could see. Lined with trees, it had a contained but welcoming look to it. None of the homes in town had yards this big, and I thought to myself how much I would have loved a yard this size to play in when I was a little girl.

The sound of rustling leaves tore me out of my daydreams, and suddenly scared, I grabbed the shovel. Holding it up and ready to swing at whatever might be out here, I slowly backed away toward the front of the house only to run into something hard.

I turned around prepared to defend myself and nearly fainted. There standing in front of me was Alexander, his eyes full of rage and a gun in his hand pointed directly at my head!

"What are you doing here?" he demanded to know, practically growling at me.

Stepping back, I gripped the handle of the shovel so tightly my palms ached and stared into his brown eyes so full of anger. Was he angry at me?

"I'm…I'm sorry. I just…I just wanted to see if you would…" I stammered out as I watched his face grow angrier by the second.

"If I would what? Why are you out here sneaking around my house? Am I suspect in your little case now?"

Suspect in my little case? What was he talking about?

"No. I mean, I was just hoping I could talk to you

about it," I tried to explain, still terrified at the gun pointed at my head.

"I don't want to talk to anyone, so just leave," he said, his voice full of venom.

Even though it went against every defensive instinct I possessed, I lowered the shovel and forced a smile. "Alexander, if you could just not point that gun at my face, maybe we could talk for a few minutes?"

As if he was deciding if he wanted to speak to me or not, he softened his expression for a moment and instead of pure anger coming at me, I saw a gentleness that I hadn't seen in him before. His brown eyes didn't glare out at me like the very sight of my face enraged him. And his shoulders lowered slightly like he was relaxing.

But then the moment was over and his eyebrows knitted, telling me he hadn't reconsidered talking to me.

He lowered his gun and frowned. "You don't want to speak to me. I can't help you."

"You might be able to. Derek told me you were a great detective when you were working in the Baltimore police, and while he might just be a local guy, he does tend to have a good sense of people."

Alexander practically sneered at me as I complimented him. "I'm not that person anymore."

"But you could be again. Great instincts don't just go away simply because you're not on the job."

He simply stared at me, brown eyes boring into mine like he was searching them for the real reason why I was lurking outside his home at dusk after getting such a cool reception at our first meeting. I saw distrust and hurt in those eyes. I didn't know why, but I wished I could explain myself better to make him see that I wasn't the person he'd taken an instant dislike to from the moment we met.

"I can't help you. You need to go."

He turned to leave, and I gently grabbed his sleeve to stop him and saw that look of anger he'd worn just a minute earlier return when he looked down where my fingers touched his shirt. Never before had I seen a look so full of rage, and I instantly backed away.

"I promise it wouldn't take too much of your time. I just have a few questions about some things I thought you could help me with.

Nearly spitting the words out, he said, "Go home, Miss McGuire. You don't belong here."

For the second time that day I'd been addressed as Miss McGuire, and this time felt no better than the first. The disdain in his voice actually hurt even more than the swipe from the nasty Widow Dunn. I hated the idea that he was no better than some small town, narrow-minded old woman with her judgmental ways and sharp tongue. I wanted to believe he was different.

Like me.

But he wasn't.

"Fine. I just wanted to get your opinion on some things involved in the Geneva Woodward case, and I thought you might want to help. I'm sorry I was mistaken."

He stood there just staring at me after my outburst, but I wanted to be anywhere else in the world than standing there being judged in his backyard. Pushing past him, I dropped the shovel and hurried back to my car as tears welled in my eyes. I hated when I got so angry that I cried. It made me feel weak, and I didn't want to be weak.

And even more, I didn't want him to see that he and

his nastiness had affected me that much. I wasn't some weepy little thing he could just dismiss without even the pretense of respect or kindness. I was a grown woman who had dug her heels in and fought to get her life back together after having it all fall apart around me more than once.

I was someone who wanted to find the truth and was tough enough to do whatever was necessary.

This case was far more than the simple one Derek thought it was. If Alexander didn't want to help me prove that, then fine. I'd do it on my own.

As I sat in my car with my hands gripping the steering wheel in anger at how he'd acted, I was more resolved than ever to see this case through to the end. Damn him and his anti-social bullshit. I'd work on this case alone, just like I would have if I never met him.

Wiping the tears from my eyes, I started my Jeep and drove away from Alexander Montero and his unwelcoming house. By the time I got home, I'd cursed him up and down three ways to Sunday and felt much better for it.

This girl didn't need him anyway. If he wanted to stay secluded and alone all closed up out there in his dark house, then he was welcome to it. I didn't need his help, and I wouldn't ask again.

TOO KEYED UP to even attempt to sit in my house, I headed over to my father's bar for a good stiff drink and the hope of finding something to take my mind off my troubles. I found him behind the bar waiting on customers instead of his usual weeknight bartender, Josie.

Plopping myself down on a barstool, I blew the air out of my lungs and ordered a drink. "Give me a shot, please."

My father's eyebrows shot up in a look of surprise. I rarely drank anything stronger than beer, and when I did, it never failed to make me even chattier than I normally was. I didn't care, though. I was in a mood and I wanted a drink that would make me forget how rotten Alexander Montero had been.

"Something wrong, honey?"

He placed the shot glass full of whisky in front of me and watched as I tossed it back. Wincing as the alcohol burned my throat the whole way down, I put the empty glass down on the bar.

"Another, please."

He poured the second shot of whisky and positioned the glass on the bar in front of me again but without repeating his question. I drank the shot down as fast as I had the first one, thankful it didn't burn as much this time.

Feeling better or at least looser, I leaned back and pushed the shot glass away from me. "Thanks, Dad. I'm good now."

"Want to talk about what's on your mind before that whisky really hits you and I have to carry you upstairs so you can sleep it off?"

"It's two shots. I'm not a total lightweight, so I think I can handle that much alcohol. Anyway, my anger level will probably just negate any really great effects from it, so you don't have to worry."

Curious at my mention of being angry, he leaned against the bar and asked, "Who's got you this mad at them?"

I didn't want to talk about Alexander and how rude he'd been, so I dodged the question with one of my own. "How do you know it's a person? Maybe it's work. Maybe it's the case."

My father leveled his gaze on me for a long moment and then shook his head. "Nope. I know you. It's a person."

As the whisky began to hit me, I had to fight the urge to talk more than I should, so I waved him off, dismissing his claim. "That's crazy. Anger is the same whether it's at a person or at some inanimate thing."

"It's anything but crazy. I know my daughter, so what's going on that's got you so furious tonight?"

He wasn't going to let me off the hook on this, so I took a deep breath in and attempted to be as vague as possible. I didn't want to admit that a near perfect stranger, a person I'd only met twice, had such an effect on me.

"I'm just frustrated with this case and hoped to get some help with it, but the person I wanted to help me doesn't want to. It's not a big deal."

"Looks like a pretty big deal to me. Maybe they had something else to do and couldn't help," he said in that steady voice that told me he felt he needed to talk me down.

But his unknowing defense of Alexander only served to irritate me more.

"He was just sitting out there at that house of his all alone. I doubt he had anything else to do. He just didn't want to help."

A quizzical look settled into his face, and he narrowed his eyes in confusion. "Who are we talking about, Poppy? I thought you meant Derek."

I shook my head, and the room swam around me. "No, not Derek. Derek's fine. Derek's just as he's always been. He's Derek."

"Well, I'm glad we got that straightened out. So if it's not Derek who's gotten your Irish up, who is the poor soul on the receiving end of your wrath?"

Muttering, I said his name. "Alexander Montero."

My father's eyes lit up. "The retired Baltimore detective?"

"How do you know about him?" I asked, confused as to whether I'd missed something of the conversation because of the two shots of whisky I'd drank entirely too fast.

"He's come in here a couple times to have a drink. Likes to drink single malt scotch. Much better than the stuff you just gulped down."

"When did he come in here?"

My father thought about my question for a moment and said, "The first time was two nights ago, and he was back last night. He doesn't say much, though, but he's pleasant enough. He's got a '69 Mustang Boss I'd practically kill to get my hands on. Did you see it when you went out to his house?"

"Yeah, it's nice. You spoke to him?"

Shaking his head, my father poured me a cup of coffee behind the bar and set it down in front of me. "Not really, but Derek and Dominick were here and we got to talking about old times and your mother, so he didn't really have much to add to the conversation."

Taking a sip of coffee, I let the warmth ease my throat and said, "Well, I'm glad you got the nice version of him because I got the cranky guy who points a gun at people."

My father's eyes opened wide. "He pointed a gun at you? If I had known he was that kind of person, I wouldn't have bought him a drink that first night. Are you okay?"

"Yeah," I said with a shrug. "He didn't shoot me. He just pointed a gun at me because he found me in the back of his house."

"He found you sneaking around his house and pointed a gun at you. Sounds like he might have had good reason to do that, Poppy."

I took another sip of my coffee and felt my whisky buzz begin to fade away. "Whose side are you on, Dad? I wasn't sneaking anywhere."

"I didn't realize there were sides, and you know I'm always on yours when there are any to be taken. I'm just saying that you might have given him a start and as a former cop, his first reaction would be to reach for his gun if he found a stranger on his property."

I always hated when my father made sense and it could be used against me. I didn't want to argue with him about Alexander and how I may have been out of line walking around his house without asking, so I kept my mouth shut and merely gave him the smile that told him I knew he was right but I didn't want to admit it.

Thankfully, my father knew me well and didn't force the issue. I loved that about him. I didn't need a lecture to make me see I may have messed up with Alexander when I went out to his place.

Finishing my coffee, I leaned over the bar and gave my father a kiss on the cheek. "Thanks for everything, Dad. I'm sober enough to walk home, so you don't have to let me stay upstairs."

"There's a murderer on the loose in Sunset Ridge,

Poppy. Do you think it's a good idea to walk alone in the dark, even if it is only a couple blocks? Let me walk you home."

"Geneva's murderer isn't going to come after me, Dad. He or she had a relationship with her that made them want to kill her. I'll be perfectly fine walking to my house. Don't worry. I bet my life on it."

His face twisted into a horrified grimace, and he shook his head. "Not funny, Elizabeth. Not funny."

I winked at him and stepped down off the barstool. "It was a little funny, but seriously, don't worry. I'll be fine."

As I walked toward the door to leave, he yelled, "Call me when you get home."

I spun around and laughed at his protective father act. "Seriously?"

"Humor me. If you don't, then I'll have to close the bar and come over to make sure you're okay."

A few people at the bar booed at his suggestion, and swiveling my head back and forth to look at the ten or so customers he had that night, I smiled. "I will, Dad. Don't worry, though. It'll be okay."

Chapter Seven

MY ALARM WOKE me out of a sound sleep, and rolling over to shut it off, I opened my eyes to see it was nearly eight in the morning. Confused because my alarm was always set for an hour earlier, I focused and saw I'd hit snooze four times already.

Two shots of whisky had never hit me that hard. I must have been exhausted to sleep through my alarm. Fully rested, I set my mind to working on the Geneva Woodward case and headed off to the shower to start my day. An hour later, I was ready to begin truly figuring out who the murderer was.

I heard a knock on my kitchen door and expected to find my father standing there to check up on me. Ready with a snappy comeback to his jokes about me being hung over, I opened the door to see not my father but Alexander standing there with a coffee from The Grounds in his hand.

"Good morning. I come bringing a peace offering," he said with a smile that looked genuine and made snapping at him impossible.

"Good morning. You're the last person I expected to see when I opened the door."

"May I come in?"

I considered the idea of grabbing the coffee out of his hand since I could smell it was my favorite dark roast blend and then slamming the door in his face, but I couldn't. I wasn't that kind of person, even if I still didn't like how he'd acted toward me on the two occasions we'd been around one another.

"Sure. Please come in," I said as I opened the door wide and stepped back to allow him to pass.

Closing the door, I turned to see him offering me my coffee. "I thought you might like this."

I inhaled the delicious smell of my favorite coffee. The man certainly knew how to come bearing gifts first thing in the morning. But then it dawned on me. We'd never had coffee together, so how did he know this was my favorite? Lucky guess?

Taking it from him, I asked, "How did you know how to get it?"

Alexander gave me a sly smile that somehow made him even more attractive. "I'm a detective. It's my job to know things like that."

Oh, he was entirely too confident.

I offered him a seat at my kitchen table and took a drink of the dark roast coffee made exactly as I liked it— two sugars, three creamers, and ice. In fact, the temperature told me he'd gotten the number of ice cubes right too. Three. But how?

"So Mr. I'm a Detective, how did you know to get it just the right temperature and exactly the way I take it? I'm a pretty particular coffee drinker."

Another smile, but this one was slow to spread across his face and so charming I almost looked away, worried I might blush at any moment. Almost. I didn't look away, though, because I wanted the answer to my question.

"I pay attention to what goes on around me. I was sitting in The Grounds one morning when you came in and ordered that very particular cup of coffee. It stayed with me from that day."

Still quite shocked at his even being there in my kitchen, I leveled my gaze on him and tried to determine if he was telling the truth or just trying to charm me. "So you're telling me that you remembered the exact way I take my coffee, even though you didn't know me from a can of paint…when did you hear this anyway?"

"A week or so ago."

"From a week ago, when I was a perfect stranger to you and simply some person ordering a coffee, you remembered that this morning and got me my coffee just like I like it?"

He chuckled. "Yes, and the girl behind the counter knew how you took your coffee when I told her it was for you. I'd forgotten how many ice cubes, if we're being honest."

I took another sip of coffee and couldn't help but smile. He probably charmed the pants off Jennie. And he probably didn't have to remember anything about how I took my coffee because he just told her it was for me.

Detective indeed.

"So what are you doing here, Alexander?"

The smile slowly faded, and after taking a drink from his cup, he lowered his head slightly and looked me directly in the eyes. "I came to apologize for what happened last night."

This guy had the most delicious brown eyes I'd ever seen. Brown like expensive milk chocolate, and at that moment, I felt myself getting lost in those eyes.

Snap out of it, Poppy! This isn't some high school date. If he's willing to make peace, maybe you can get his help on the case, so get your head out of the clouds and say something!

I turned away to break our shared gaze and then looked back at him. "I guess I should apologize too. I should have handled that differently. I'm sorry."

"I am too. I shouldn't have pulled my gun on you, and for that, I'm truly sorry. I have no excuse."

Something in those eyes of his told me he did have an excuse but he wasn't going to tell me. All the better because I sensed hurt lay behind how he acted.

Extending my hand, I offered my own olive branch. "No harm, no foul. Maybe if we pretend like we're meeting for the first time we can put those other times behind us. Hi, I'm Poppy. Nice to meet you."

That slow smile returned, and he took my hand in his to shake it. "Hi, Poppy. I'm Alexander, but my friends call me Alex."

"Hi, Alex."

And with those two words, everything between us changed. I didn't know why or how, but suddenly I had a feeling that he would become one of the most important people in my life. At the same time, I felt like I'd known him my entire life, even though I'd just met him days before and this was the first time we'd ever spoken more than a handful of civil words to each other.

Strangely, our conversation came to an abrupt halt after reintroducing ourselves to one another. He seemed content to sit there next to me and drink his coffee in silence, so I took the opportunity to study him as he seemed to have studied me already.

He was definitely a good looking man. I didn't need

to spend much time studying him to see that. Dark, thick hair and those delicious brown eyes that told anyone who looked into them that there was a story in his past gave him an exotic feel. With the last name Montero, he was likely Italian or maybe Greek. Sunset Ridge didn't have many citizens with those ethnic backgrounds, which made him stand out even more.

I let my gaze drift over him as he sat there silently and couldn't help notice his hands. Strong looking, they were bigger than even my father's working class hands and had long fingers. I'd noted that he wasn't married the first time we'd met because of the lack of a wedding band, but now that I sat right next to him, I could see the lighter skin where it had sat on his ring finger until recently.

So where was Mrs. Montero? Was she the woman I'd read about in the obituary from nearly five years ago? Possibly, but if that was the case, why was the mark where the wedding band had been still so clear? Five years was a long time to wear a wedding band for a wife who'd died.

I wanted to ask about his wife, if only to say I was sorry because it seemed like I should and if that wedding band mark was any indication, he still hurt. But I didn't. Alex and I were practically strangers, and strangers didn't pry like that.

At least this stranger didn't.

If he was sitting with one of those committee ladies and they had any inkling of a wife in his past, the poor man would now be dodging questions left and right about her. Those Founders' Day ladies were nothing if not nosy.

The thought of Alex stuck in a room with those four

made me smile, and I looked up from staring at his hands to see he had seen where I was looking. Quickly, I turned away to avoid his gaze, feeling oddly embarrassed.

"You have a nice house here. Very cozy."

I turned back to see him scanning my kitchen, as if he were studying it like I'd been studying him. "Thank you. I like it."

"It's a big house for just one person."

I wanted to ask how he was so sure I lived alone, but he didn't even have to be a half-way decent detective to know that. A few minutes with my father the other night at the bar and he likely had my entire life story.

"I guess," I mumbled, sort of hating how awkward things had gotten between us already.

He didn't continue the conversation, but that seemed to be the type of person he was. Talk about opposites. I was what my father had always called a Chatty Cathy, but Alex parsed out words like they cost him money every time one came out of his mouth.

Sitting quietly for a few more minutes, the question that had been on my mind earlier before I got lost in those eyes of his and the idea that his past was some kind of tragedy came back to me.

Why was he here?

Breaking the uncomfortable silence, I asked, "Alex, why did you come here today? I mean, you could have just apologized and then left or simply called me to say you were sorry. Instead you come here and say you're sorry and then say little else. What are you doing here?"

I cringed at how blunt that sounded. I never meant to phrase things so succinctly. They just came out that way. Before I could apologize, though, he nodded and began to speak again.

"I like how forthright you are, Poppy. That kind of frankness is refreshing, so I'll return the favor. I've heard a number of things about you, and all of them point to someone who's smart. You're different than everyone else I've met in this town. I also know this is the first time you're working with Derek on one of his cases. To be honest, I know why he likes to have you around, but I have to believe you want to work with him on this Geneva Woodward case because you're a detective in your heart and not because you have some secret love for the brother of our police chief."

A mixture of stunned disbelief at how much Alex knew about me and amusement at the thought of my having any romantic feelings for Derek washed over me. My brain felt like it short-circuited, and not knowing what to say, I let out a laugh as the thought of Derek and me settled into my mind.

"Did I say something funny?" Alex asked, his gaze intently focused on me now.

"No. I guess I just got sidetracked by the idea of Derek and me together since, to be honest, I felt a little exposed by the rest of what you said."

"So no secret romance between you and him?" he asked with a smile that told me he was trying to make things less uncomfortable.

I shook my head and screwed my face into an expression that was meant to show my distaste for anything like that with Derek Hampton. "No. He's nice, but he's not my type."

"I had a feeling. As for the other things I said, I didn't mean to make you feel like I've been prying into your personal life. Your father loves you a great deal and he likes to brag about you. I will admit I checked into what he said and found he wasn't exaggerating. Your job at The Bottom Line might be beneath you, but you're good at it. See? You are a detective in your heart."

The reality of how little progress I'd made in finding out who'd murdered Geneva or even proving that it wasn't a robbery gone wrong like Derek thought made my shoulders sag, and I lowered my head to admit the truth. "I'm not a very good detective, it seems. I haven't gotten very far with this case."

"You came out to my house to ask me a few questions last night before I ran you off like some criminal, so I have a proposition to make you. I'd like to help you with the Geneva Woodward case, if you'll take my assistance."

Once again, Alex Montero had surprised me. "Why would you want to help me instead of helping Derek? He's the actual policeman. I'm just an amateur investigator with wild ideas. Or at least that's what Derek thinks."

Leaning back against the chair, Alex smiled. "From what I heard that day in the office, he's got what happened to that woman all figured out. He wouldn't be interested in my help."

"You're a real detective, and you want to work with me? Why?" I asked, still in disbelief he'd want to partner up with me.

"Because you have good instincts, and I agree with you. This wasn't a robbery gone south. Someone murdered that woman, and I'm guessing it was a crime of passion. Or maybe it was premeditated, but whatever happened, it wasn't some stranger caught at the wrong place at the wrong time like Derek wants to believe."

"Really? Why do you think that it wasn't a thief breaking in and getting caught?" I asked while inside I rejoiced at the fact that a Baltimore detective actually believed as I did about the case.

"Because I'm like you. I listen to what the people in this town say as I sit next to them while they drink their morning coffee or stand in line with them at the Post Office. They've seen me enough times in town to not pay any attention to me anymore since my newness has worn off, so it's the perfect chance to listen to what they have to say without them noticing."

"Have you heard anything interesting?"

"I've heard a lot of interesting things in the time I've lived around here, but nothing about this case. Derek mentioned that you were talking to people about it, though, so have you found anything yet?"

I thought about all I'd heard and sighed. "Yes and no. I think some of it may be useful."

"Tell me."

I took a mouthful of coffee to finish the cup and sat up in my chair. "Okay. So far I've spoken to her next door neighbor Michelle Steadman—well, Shelley—and found out that Geneva had begun to receive nighttime visits from some mystery man about a month ago. That would fit in with what my father told me about her coming around to see him before that."

"So Geneva had an active private life."

"The problem is that she always acted like she didn't. Before I began asking around, I'd never heard anything about Geneva Woodward like Shelley and my father said."

"Okay. What else?"

"I had a meeting with the Founders' Day committee the other day for a piece I'm writing for *The Eagle* and I found out a lot about Geneva there. For one thing, all those women didn't seem like they'd shed even a single tear when they found out poor Geneva had been strangled to death."

"Maybe because one of them is the one who did it? Maybe they're covering for one of their own?" he asked.

I sat back as my brain processed what he'd said. "I never thought about it that way. I don't know."

"Well, we'll keep it in mind. What else did you find out at the meeting?"

"A lot of gossip about Geneva basically being the town trollop. They claimed she'd had affairs with a number of well-known men in town. When I told Derek about that, he said he'd heard the rumors before her death and had already checked out the husbands and their wives and found out they all had solid alibis."

"Is there any reason to not believe that?" Alex asked with a look of concern I couldn't place.

"No. Why?"

"Because if there isn't, you can disregard that piece of information. While it may be useful to understanding Geneva's character, it doesn't point to any of them being suspects. So we can forget about them but remember what they said about her, assuming we believe Derek."

"Okay." I mentally went through my notes about the meeting and said, "I think that's about it. Lots of talking pretty poorly about the dead, which isn't surprising with that group, but not much else."

"So our best lead so far is Geneva's next door neighbor, Shelley. Is she sure the person coming to see Geneva at night was a man?"

I nodded, remembering how insistent she'd been that poor Geneva was having some kind of midnight rendezvous a few times a week. Then that comment the mayor's wife had made about the police at her house jumped into my mind.

"There was one more thing. The First Lady, I mean Eleanor Girard, the former mayor's wife, said that she knew for a fact that the police had been called to Geneva's house a number of times, but when I told Derek about that, he said there wasn't even one call to her house logged in on the station's computer system."

"Interesting. Is there any reason to believe she lied or exaggerated?"

I thought about the woman who insisted on being called the First Lady even now after her husband left office months ago. "Everything about Eleanor Girard is an exaggeration, but I don't know if I'd say she'd lie. She is a politician's wife, though, so maybe."

Alex said nothing for a long while, which made me feel like he'd listened to what I'd said and was trying to find a way to tell me I really wasn't very good at this detective thing. I didn't have much to go on yet, but in my defense, this was my first case. If things were moving slowly, I wanted to believe I'd get better as things continued.

Finally, I broke the silence, unable to keep quiet any longer. "I know it doesn't seem like much, but I still believe she wasn't killed by some stranger."

He shook his head and smiled. "Please don't take my silence for anything other than my thinking things through. It's just how I work. As for not having much, I think you're wrong. Shelley is definitely worth another look because she can give us some information about what Geneva was doing at the time she was murdered in the days preceding her death, and what the ladies of the Founders' Day committee thought may be useful too."

"You know what's been on my mind ever since I started investigating this? The picture all these people paint of Geneva is so different than what I'd always thought of her. She always seemed so distant and cold, yet all these women tell stories that contradict that."

"So either you're wrong or they are. Which is it?"

"I'm not sure. I guess there's a good chance they're right and I didn't really know her at all," I admitted.

He stood from the table and threw his coffee cup in the garbage. "Well, then let's see what we can find out."

I looked up at him standing there waiting for me to join him to set out to find who had killed Geneva Woodward and still wondered what he was doing helping me. "Why are you doing this, Alex?"

That look of hurt settled into his eyes once again, and after a long pause he said, "I need an excuse to get out of my house and join the land of the living and you need help. So let's get started."

I heard sadness in his voice when he said *land of the living*. As he stood smiling down at me, I had a sense his happiness was forced.

Whatever the pain of his past was, he hadn't shaken it yet.

Chapter Eight

ALEX AND I walked up the sidewalk toward Shelley Steadman's front porch and stopped at the bottom of the stairs. I figured I should warn him about her. "Just a head's up. Shelley's probably going to try to get you to be husband number four. She's like that."

Grinning like what I'd said amused him, he said, "Then I guess I'll be the one asking the questions today. You'd be surprised at how loose people's tongues become when they have something else on their minds."

I had a feeling he got that a lot, so I didn't fight him on the idea of him taking the lead with her. Whatever it took to get her to either tip her hand and show herself as the killer or reveal some clue to go on about Geneva's mystery man, I was all for it.

He knocked on the door as I leaned in and whispered, "Oh, I forgot to tell you. Derek texted me that the coroner is putting the time of death between midnight and three Monday morning."

Just as the door began to open, he turned his head and winked. "Good to know. I'm curious to know where Shelley was during that time."

I opened my mouth to ask why he'd already decided she was a person of interest, but I didn't get a chance before Shelley herself was standing in front of us. It took her no time to decide she liked Alex, and the happy expression on her face instantly showed just how much.

"Good morning! What can I do for you on this beautiful day?" she said in almost a purring sound as she extended her hand toward Alex. "And who might you be?"

He shook her hand and flashed her a smile like he knew exactly how to manipulate her interest. "My name is Alex Montero, Mrs. Steadman. I think you already know Miss McGuire. Do you have a few minutes to speak to us?"

Shelley's gaze drifted up and down Alex's body, finally settling on his face. With a big toothy grin, she corrected him. "I'm not married, Alex, and I'm happy to speak to you about anything you'd like."

"Thank you. I promise we won't take up much of your time," he said in a purring voice that matched hers as he stepped over the threshold into her foyer.

I followed along feeling like the ugly stepchild, mumbling, "It's nice to see you again too, Shelley."

But if she heard my snide remark, she ignored it. Her attention was entirely on Alex, who she had taken hold of and was now walking arm in arm with toward her parlor. For his part, he seemed completely at home with her fawning all over him, so I just hung back and did my best to be invisible since he obviously had a plan for how to get her to loosen her tongue, as he'd said.

She offered him a seat on her settee next to her and slid over toward him so she was practically sitting on his lap. "What can I do for you, Alex? Are you helping the police with solving poor Geneva's murder?"

"I am, so any help you can give today would be so

appreciated. We just have a few questions."

His use of the word we made Shelley look over toward me as I stood next to her fireplace fiddling with three porcelain monkeys that sat on the mantle. "I almost didn't see you there, Poppy. I think it's wonderful that you have a man like Alex to help you with your investigation. I'm sure the wretched man who committed this horrible crime will be caught now."

"Yes, it's wonderful to have a wonderful man like Alex by my side," I said with as much civility as I could muster. What I really wanted to tell her was that I didn't appreciate her demeaning me as a woman and treating me like I needed some man around to solve this case.

But I didn't since the entire time Shelley was turned around speaking to me he was giving me the "don't mess this up" look. I didn't much appreciate that either.

Turning back toward her new favorite man, she placed her hand on his bicep and purred, "Would you like something to drink? I'll be right back with some iced tea and cookies I know you'll just devour."

And with that, she rushed out of the room, leaving me standing there glaring at him. I took three giant steps in his direction and stopped as my anger bubbled up inside me.

"I don't know which is worse. Shelley treating me like I'm some helpless female tied to the railroad tracks who needs to be rescued by a big, wonderful man like you, or you giving me that look like I'm a complete idiot who doesn't see exactly what you're up to."

My outburst surprised him, and for a moment he said nothing. All the better. I didn't want to argue with him. I just wanted him to know I wasn't a complete social klutz.

When he did speak, he hadn't turned off his smarminess better suited to Shelley. "Poppy, I just wanted to make sure you knew what I was doing."

I leaned down close to him so she wouldn't hear and whispered, "Don't use that sappy voice with me. That may work with the likes of her, but it doesn't with me. How about you remember I'm not tagging along as your assistant or gal Friday here? And don't treat me like I'm some accessory, like a new tie or cufflinks."

If what I said earlier had surprised him, now he was downright stunned. I stepped back to my post near the fireplace before his eyes returned to their normal size and folded my arms across my chest. I didn't want to hear anything more from him or give him a chance to think of something nice to say.

Shelley came back to the parlor pushing a cart with a glass pitcher of iced tea, three already filled glasses, and a plate of sugar cookies. Parking it a few feet away from Alex on the settee, she handed him a glass of iced tea and then turned to offer me one too. At least I wouldn't have to stand there without something to do and watch the two of them have a nice little snack while they fawned over one another.

"I have to use a cart because I can't carry trays anymore. I have problems holding anything after too many years working. Thankfully, I don't have to worry about that anymore," Shelley explained to Alex as she offered him a cookie. "Please take one. They melt in your mouth. I made them myself."

"I love sugar cookies," he cooed as he took one from the plate and bit into it. "Oh, they're delicious, Shelley."

When I couldn't stand to watch her moon over him eating her sugar cookie any longer, I said loudly, "So

Shelley, we're here to talk about the mystery man you told me about the other day when I was here."

And had no iced tea or cookies offered to me.

Both Alex and Shelley looked over at me for a moment like I was some rude intruder on a private moment, but he quickly recovered and nodded. "Poppy's right. We do need to get down to business, no matter how tempting your cookies are. Do you remember anything more about the man you saw going into Geneva's house?"

She took a moment to think, or maybe it was to gaze into his eyes, but then she said, "I can tell you he was tall, dark haired, and well-built. Not as well-built as you, but definitely in shape."

Alex pressed her further. "Do you think you can be even more detailed?"

Shelley slid her hand down over his bicep again and sighed. "You know how when you see an attractive man and you just know under his clothes there's an incredible body?" She paused to see if her arrow had hit its mark, and when she saw Alex smile, she continued. "I don't think he had that kind of body but he wasn't fat, old, and flabby."

As much as my new partner might have thought this was helping, we weren't getting anywhere. Well, unless Alex's aim was to be fawned over like the star quarterback after the big game. If that were the case, he and Shelley were definitely getting the job done.

Even though I knew it risked ruining his whole plan, I chimed in and asked, "How many times did you see this man, Shelley? When did the visits begin?"

She turned on the settee and flashed me a look of disgust. "I saw him no less than six times. As for when the visits began, I want to say it was about a month ago. Yeah, a month ago sounds right."

"And what was he dressed in?" I asked, feeling like if I didn't get all my questions in at once, she'd turn back to flirting with Alex and we'd never move forward.

She looked up toward the ceiling and with an audible sigh said, "I don't know. It was always dark. I want to say he was in dark clothes, but I don't know for sure."

"Was he wearing a coat? It was cold a few weeks ago," I said as I thought about how low the temperatures had stayed until early April this year.

Shelley shook her head. "No, I don't think he was wearing a coat the times I saw him. But that doesn't mean he didn't when I didn't see him."

I felt my face twist into an expression of disgust at her unhelpfulness. This woman wasn't useful at all.

"Shelley, can we see where you were standing so we can know exactly what you saw?" Alex asked in a far too accommodating voice for my taste.

Clearly excited by his suggestion, she chirped, "Of course. Follow me."

Shelley led us upstairs to a bedroom and the window that looked out over Geneva's backyard. Pulling back the curtains, she pointed to the house next door. "I was standing right here. I saw the man go in through the back door there."

Alex and I took our place next to her and looked down into the yard. In a low voice, he said, "There's an alley way behind these houses."

Then he turned around and asked Shelley, "I'm thinking you weren't standing here just gazing out the window, right? How did you come to see him on those nights?"

Smiling, she answered, "Well, this is my bedroom and I was lying in bed that first night and heard a strange noise outside. So I jumped out of bed and went to the window and there he was walking up poor Geneva's back stairs."

"When was that exactly?" Alex asked before I could get the words out of my mouth.

"A month ago, like I said."

I began to say that was March and it was unlikely she'd have her window open to hear a noise outside, unless it was really loud, but Alex cut me off after just a few words.

"If I go outside, will you tell me if you see any resemblance as I walk up the back stairs?"

"Sure!" Shelley agreed, thrilled to be a part of Alex's playacting.

"Okay, open the window and give me a minute. Poppy, can you help me?"

Alex tugged my arm to follow him, so I reluctantly left Shelley before I could get some real answers out of her. Pressing his finger to his lips to keep me quiet, he walked down the stairs and out the back door toward Geneva's house. When we reached her steps, he looked up toward Shelley's bedroom window and smiled.

"Tell me everything me standing here reminds you of, Shelley."

Under my breath, I mumbled, "How much do you want to bet she's going to say the balcony scene from Romeo and Juliet?"

"He wasn't as tall as you, Alex," Shelley yelled down. "But he had a body like yours."

"Did she want to jump his bones too?" I teased as

Alex took a step toward Geneva's porch.

"Anything else, Shelley?" he asked her as we continued what felt like busy work or an excuse to give his admirer more chances to check him out.

She leaned out her window and gazed longingly down at him for a few moments before shaking her head. "No. Nothing else."

"Did he have to wait to be let in?"

I hadn't thought of that and looked up toward Shelley, eager to hear the answer. She seemed to think about it for a moment and then said, "He might have knocked once or twice, but that night she was killed, he didn't knock. I remember that."

"Okay. We'll meet you in the parlor."

He waited until Shelley had left the window and turned to face me. "I bet you're wondering what the purpose for all that was."

"Are you a mind reader too, Mr. Wonderful?" I said with a chuckle.

"Shelley's not telling the truth. I just wanted to see if we could get her to slip up. I think she was in her bedroom the night of the murder, though. Whether she stayed there all night or walked over to Geneva's to strangle her is a different story. And yes, before you say anything, I caught what she said about hearing a noise outside that made her get up and look. Since it was March then, I'm willing to bet she didn't have her window open, so hearing a man walk up these steps was unlikely. Did you hear what noise they made when I walked up them?"

Sheepishly, I admitted I hadn't. "No, but Geneva might have gotten them fixed."

"If you hadn't been so concerned about how much

Shelley likes me, you would have noticed they made no noise when I stepped on them and they're old wooden steps. She didn't get them fixed because there was nothing wrong with them to fix."

Embarrassed, I looked down toward the white painted wood steps and nodded. "Point taken. I don't know why her fawning all over you bugs me."

"Because her type of female is the opposite of yours. She equates happiness with a man. Today, I'm that man, but I'm sure there will be a delivery guy to take my place in her heart tomorrow. You're not like that, so her behavior bothers you."

"Do you have an answer for everything?" I asked, frustrated by how right his explanation was.

One of his slow smiles lit up his face, and he began walking back toward Shelley's house. "No. I still don't know who killed poor Geneva."

"Now you're sounding like Shelley with that poor Geneva stuff," I joked as I followed him.

She met us at the back door wearing a big smile. As she pushed open the screen door to let us in, she asked, "Did anything I say help?"

I let Alex answer her since if I did I might let what I was thinking slip out. Still smarting from knowing that I'd let myself be irritated by her behavior even though it shouldn't have affected me in the slightest, I decided it might be better to let Alex do the talking with Shelley from that point on. I might not like it, but he did have a way of getting her to talk.

By the time we got back to the parlor, Shelley was back to flirting and I was back to rolling my eyes. I might have been able to keep quiet, but I wasn't capable of totally turning off my reactions. Not that it mattered.

She didn't look at me from the moment she laid eyes on him at the back door. I could have lifted half a dozen expensive knick-knacks as I trailed behind them, and she would have never known she was so distracted.

"So do you have any idea who did this horrible crime? I haven't felt safe since the whole thing happened, so I truly hope you catch him. It can be quite frightening living all alone in this big house with no one to protect me, and just knowing someone killed poor Geneva right next door is just so upsetting."

"Not yet," Alex said as he took a bite of a sugar cookie and washed it down with a gulp of iced tea. "But you've been very helpful. Thank you, Shelley."

Once again pawing him, this time on his hand, she said in that purring voice that grated on my last nerve, "It's my pleasure. I just wish I could remember more about that man visiting her all those nights. I love the idea of midnight rendezvous, don't you?"

Alex took a pen and a piece of paper out of his windbreaker and wrote a phone number on it. "If you remember anything else, please call. Anything at all might be helpful."

Shelley nearly ripped the paper from his fingers as he handed it to her. Her eyes fixed on the number, and she held that piece of scrap paper like it was something precious. "I will. I genuinely want to help, so I'm going to think about all those nights I saw that man and call when I remember something."

"Please do."

Standing, he took her hand in his and shook it, but not the way he'd shake a friend or acquaintance's hand. More like he cradled her hand. Whatever he was doing, it worked because Shelley looked like she was about to melt.

"It was a pleasure meeting you, Shelley. Thank you for all your help."

"Yes, thank you," I chimed in as she walked us toward the front door. "You've been so gracious to speak about this twice, especially during this time of mourning for your friend."

Shelley flashed me a smile and then seemed to remember that it was, in fact, just days since her dear friend had been strangled to death. Putting on a sad face, she said, "I just want to help bring him to justice."

"Thank you, Shelley. Remember, if you think of anything, just call that number," Alex said in that smarmy voice again.

"I will. I promise," she purred one last time as she closed the door behind us.

"I really hate that voice you put on for her, you know that? Please don't ever use that voice on me or I'll be forced to do something you might not like," I said as we walked toward the sidewalk that ran up and down Cherry Street.

He looked back at Shelley's house and then at me. "You and Shelley are two entirely different people. I would never use that voice on you because it wouldn't work. On Shelley, as you can see, it works."

"And what's with giving her your phone number? You better prepare yourself because she's going to be your own personal stalker. I realize I'm new at this, but a little advice, Alex. Don't give a woman like that your number, unless you want to hear from her early and often."

Stopping, he grinned like a man who had some top secret only he knew and said, "I gave her Derek's office number. If she thinks of anything, she'll be calling the police. She didn't recognize the number, so we can assume she wasn't the person who called the police, assuming those calls ever happened."

Damn, he was good. I had to admit it. The guy knew what he was doing, and I felt like a novice.

Grudgingly, I admitted what he likely already knew. "I'm pretty green about all of this. Maybe it would be better if you just investigated this on your own and I went back to my life of writing the social page for *The Eagle* and digging up dirt on pseudo-celebrities."

"You aren't green. You have good instincts, Poppy. You're just more sincere than I am. That's why I can deal with someone like Shelley in the way I had to and not be bothered in the least. She saw me as a potential mate, so I treated her the same. It's not who I am. It's just what worked with her."

As we walked down Cherry Street, I said, "I can't imagine being like that. Not that there's anything wrong with it. You used the cues she was giving off and ran with them. I've just never been a very good actress. My mother used to tell me I wore my emotions right on my sleeve and she could always see exactly what I was feeling by the expression on my face."

With a serious look in his eyes, he said, "There's nothing wrong with being like that, Poppy. It's who you are. It just makes us exact opposites. Who knows? Maybe that will make us great partners too."

I liked that idea. I may have been green, but I knew good detective work when I saw it, and that was Alex. If I could learn from him, maybe I would someday be as good as him.

He tapped me on the arm and pointed toward the

end of the street. "Let's take a look at the alley way behind the house. I'm sure the police thoroughly checked it out, but I want to see it for myself."

"Sure."

As I walked with him toward the alley way behind Geneva's house, I couldn't help but be impressed by my new partner. We may have been complete opposites, but for what it was worth, I liked to think that maybe he was right and I did have good instincts.

Chapter Nine

A N HOUR LATER, I sat at a table in the back of The Grounds while Alex waited in line for our drinks. The coffee shop was unusually busy for midday, and I had a few minutes by myself to think about what information Shelley had given us. Too bad I couldn't get her oversexed divorcee act out of my head.

Alex was right. A woman like her had nothing in common with someone like me. I couldn't imagine acting like she had, but there hadn't been an ounce of shame evident in her at any time we were there with her.

Shelley's desperate housewife performance wasn't the only thing I couldn't stop thinking about. The way Alex had handled her so expertly replayed in my mind, and I had to admit the more I thought about it, the more I wasn't sure how I felt about him being like that. Even more, did I know anything about who Alex really was? He said he wasn't the man he pretended to be to get what we needed out of Shelley, but who was he?

"You look a million miles away."

I looked up to see him standing next to the table with my coffee and a cherry danish. Jennie must have clued him into my favorite breakfast food too.

"I got you something to eat too. I know it's not really

for lunch, but I figured it might be something you'd like."

This Alex I liked and respected.

Taking my coffee from his hand, I inhaled deeply the delicious smell of dark roast. "My favorite morning drink and food? You do have a way of knowing how to ingratiate yourself with someone."

His smile faded, and his expression grew serious as he sat down. "I have a feeling you aren't comfortable with who I had to be back there, even though you said you were."

I took a sip of my coffee and decided I needed to choose my words wisely. I didn't want to offend him, but I didn't want to lie either.

"I just don't know who the real Alex Montero is, so all I have to go on is the guy who barely took the time to be polite at Derek's office and then pulled a gun on me, the guy who was standing on my porch this morning with a peace offering wanting to work with me to solve a murder, and the guy who I worried might take Shelley right there on her settee if I wasn't standing across the room."

Alex smiled and slowly lifted the coffee cup to his lips to take a drink. I couldn't help but think he was dragging the entire action out, maybe to form his answer. It came off methodical, which I had to believe was truly part of him.

"I wouldn't have taken Shelley right there on her settee."

And that was it. He said nothing else after all that.

I looked across the table at him in shock. "That's all you're going to say after that entire thing with lifting the cup slowly and then slowly putting it back down?"

"Well, I wouldn't have. She's not my type. I like my women a lot less eager."

Entirely unsatisfied with his answers, I let out a loud sigh and jammed my fork into my danish as I tried to take out my irritation on my morning pastry. This man was extraordinarily frustrating.

Alex reached across the table and gently touched my arm. Looking up, I saw that smile of his and knew he had something more to say.

"I'm just teasing you, Poppy. I'm not really that guy who was rude to you that first day or the guy who pulled a gun on you, even though you were trespassing on my property. And I'm definitely not the guy you saw at Shelley's this morning. In fact, out of all the versions of me you mentioned, I'm mostly the guy standing on your porch after he made sure to get your favorite coffee because he didn't like who he'd been last night."

I listened to everything he said and finished chewing a piece of my danish before I spoke. Unlike him, I wasn't trying to extend the other person's anticipation of what I'd say, though. I was just trying not to speak with my mouth full.

"We are two very different people, Alex. I'm afraid what you see is what you get with me. I've never been very good at subterfuge. Like I said before, I wear my emotions right on my sleeve, and every emotion I've ever had has passed over my face. My parents always claimed it's an Irish thing. You probably think of me as some simple small town person, and I guess next to you, I might be that. But this is who I am."

"I don't think that at all, but I think you do. This town isn't all you are, and I believe that with everything I know of the world. If all you were was Sunset Ridge and its mindset, you wouldn't have disagreed with Derek when he decided Geneva's murder was just some robbery gone bad."

I scoffed at his attempt to make me something I wasn't. "I disagreed with him because it was obviously not just some stranger who had come in and strangled her. Strangulation is too intimate an act. I mean, if it was just some thief, they could have just bludgeoned her to death with one of the half a dozen statues Geneva had in that room. Knowing that doesn't mean I'm not Sunset Ridge through and through."

Alex put his cup down on the table and studied my face. Within a few seconds, I felt like some butterfly under glass and began fidgeting. Smooth was definitely not my strong suit.

"Look around you, Poppy. Take a good look at the people just in this coffee shop and tell me what you see."

I scanned The Grounds and saw the usual suspects who often seemed to be there. The two twenty-something males with their laptops open who always seemed to be complaining that there should be a Starbucks in town so they wouldn't have to drink what they considered to be substandard coffee. The smattering of elderly men and women who came into the coffee shop during their shopping downtown. A few more strangers than usual rounding out the crowd.

Looking back at Alex, I said, "I see nobody who looks like me."

"That's not what I wanted you to see," he said, knitting his eyebrows into dissatisfied black slashes.

"I was teasing. I know what you meant. You think I'm not like these people, but I am, Alex. It doesn't matter that I spend most of my time daydreaming about visiting far-off places and wishing I could leave and never come back. I've lived here nearly all my life, and I come from people who lived here their entire lives."

No sooner had the words left my mouth did the realization come over me that I'd just referred to my mother. A Sunset Ridge resident all her life, except when she went away to college, Siobhan McGuire was everything this town meant to me.

"Poppy, your father isn't a small town person either. I've spoken to him. It's in him just like it's in you."

"What? What's in me and my father?" I asked defensively, disliking where this conversation had gone to.

"A curiosity for more than gossip. That's how you're different from the people in this town. How you're different from Shelley, who sat by that window every night to spy on her neighbor just because she wanted to have something to use against her. How you're different from the rest of Sunset Ridge, which seems to mostly want to talk about people instead of ideas."

"That's quite an indictment of your adopted home, don't you think?"

He shook his head solemnly. "It is what it is. I've listened to the people in this town since I moved here almost a year ago. I hear what they care about. Who's doing what to whom. Who has more money. Who's not married and why not."

His last comment hit me directly since I was one of a handful of single women above twenty-five in Sunset Ridge. I knew what people in town said about me. What they said about the others who weren't married when old women had deigned it should have happened already.

Old maids. Sad, pathetic single women left on the shelf. Destined to be single forever.

"I'm sure you've heard all about why I'm not married if you've been in town for that long," I said with a chuckle, feeling a little more defensive than I was comfortable with.

His expression still serious, despite my attempt at humor, he nodded. "I have."

Not that I wanted to hear the comments repeated again, but I'd expected more than just to hear him affirm he knew what was said about me and my single status. Unable to stop myself, I asked, "What have you heard?"

Alex remained silent for a moment, instead looking around the coffee shop, but as if he'd decided there was no point in hedging on this issue, he turned back to face me and frowned. "That you had a number of chances to get a good husband and didn't and now it might be too late. That you'll end up like the others in town who are still unmarried. That you chose to take care of your father instead of looking for a husband, and now that choice has come back to haunt you."

He stopped and then added, "That you've just about run out of time."

Swallowing hard, I tried to put on a good face. That last one hit a little too close to home. "Well, it's nice to know that the town I've lived all my life in thinks that of me."

"The women at the bank who whisper behind your back in line and the ones who gossip about you when they see you on the street are what this town is about. That's why I said you're not like them."

It hurt to think that he'd only been in Sunset Ridge

for such a short time and had heard these things about me. The same people who smiled and waved when they saw me walking to and from *The Eagle* thought so little of me that they'd consigned me to old maid status and nothing more, even though I was only in my early thirties.

The same people who had cried and wrung their hands when my mother died and then wept as she was lowered into her grave thought of me as a lost cause simply because I hadn't achieved the one thing they had in life. Forget all my other accomplishments. Forget that I had graduated at the top of my class from Sunset Ridge High School. Forget that I had graduated with honors from the University of Maryland. Forget that I was a good person and treated them like people who deserved a smile and respect when I saw them on the street.

No, all that mattered was I hadn't found a husband to take care of me. As if it was the 1950s and I needed to be taken care of.

I drank the last sips of my coffee and pushed the cup away from me. "They can think whatever they want. You can too, for that matter."

"Want to know what I think?" he asked with an intensity in his eyes I hadn't seen since the night before when he pointed his gun at my head.

I did and I didn't. After knowing him for such a short time, I respected Alex. Maybe my admiration was based on my desire to be more like him, at least when it came to solving this case. I didn't know. I just knew that whatever he said could hurt me and what I thought of him.

"Sure. Everyone else seems to have an opinion on

my life, so why shouldn't you?"

Leaning in toward me, he shrunk the distance between us until all I could focus on were those deep brown eyes so full of passion. "I think it's the twenty-first century, and if you want to stay unmarried for the rest of your life, you'd still be head and shoulders above everyone in this town. And for what it's worth, I haven't seen a man in the entire time I've been in Sunset Ridge who was worthy of you."

"Oh."

That's all I could get out I was so shocked at his answer. I didn't know what I'd expected him to say, but it hadn't been anything like that.

"So that's why I think you're nothing like the people in this town, and to me, that's a good thing. Now if we're done with the small minds surrounding us, I say we talk about how our case is going."

"Well, okay. I say we do. Where should we start?"

Grinning again, he answered, "Shelley, of course."

I couldn't stop myself from rolling my eyes. At some point soon, I truly hoped we'd get to speak to someone else in this case.

"Fine. Shelley it is. I think I should mention that when I talked to her that first time she was nothing like she was today. I got a far nastier feel from her whenever she said Geneva's name."

"Like when she used the word poor every time she said it?" he asked.

"Yeah. I don't know if they call that a Freudian slip or whatever it is, but considering the one real thing she and Geneva had in common was money, I can't help but think whenever she says poor Geneva that she's digging at her, even in death."

"From the whispers I've heard around town, I'm thinking Shelley isn't exactly of Geneva's ilk."

I couldn't help but smile at that description. "You could say that. Geneva was old money. You know the kind. They own entire towns and have streets named after their families. Shelley was new money. She became a wealthy woman after divorcing her third husband. So no, she wasn't of Geneva's ilk."

"Do you think she and Geneva had a problem that would make her want to kill her?"

Shrugging, I shook my head. "I don't know. Is jealousy enough a reason to kill someone?"

"It always has been in my experience."

Thinking back to my conversation alone with Shelley, I remembered her stopping herself from speaking ill of the dead woman. "She did almost call her a bitch when I spoke to her the other day. She didn't say anything more about it and I didn't want to push her, but there had been something between them that had ruffled dear Shelley's feathers."

"I wonder what that was."

"She also said something else to me that she didn't when you were talking to her. When it was just me, she said she saw something shiny or silver on the mystery man who was visiting Geneva. She said as she was watching from her window, she saw the glint of something silver as he walked up the stairs. Maybe a ring."

Alex thought about this for a moment and said, "Tall, dark, well-built, and wearing something silver or shiny that could be a ring. Maybe a married man. Do you think she was telling the truth?"

"I have no idea," I admitted truthfully. "My gut says

she and Geneva weren't as close as she claims they were. Does that mean she killed her? I don't know. Something upset her enough to make her want to call her a name, and I wouldn't be surprised to find out Shelley had a healthy dose of jealousy for all the things Geneva had. She's not exactly deep."

Alex laughed out loud. "No, she's not, and if her act today is any indication, she's what my father used to call hot to trot. Maybe she was jealous of what Geneva had in her mystery man and wanted it for herself."

"Hot to trot. An oldie but a goodie, and in this case, I think we can safely say it fits. So Shelley is suspect number one and the mystery man is suspect number two?" I asked, happy to be making some progress.

"Assuming there is a mystery man. All we have is Shelley's word for it, as of right now. I think we need to find someone else to corroborate her claims. Maybe one of Geneva's other neighbors?"

"Sounds like a good idea."

"Okay, let's go," he said eagerly as he stood to leave, but I grabbed his arm to stop him.

"Not yet. I think since you seem to know so much about me that I should get to know more about you."

"There's nothing more to know about me, Poppy. I'm that guy who showed up at your door with a coffee this morning."

Shaking my head, I said, "Yeah, well I think there's more, so turnabout is fair play. If we're to be partners, I think I should know more about you other than you're good at getting coffee shop waitresses to divulge my favorite blend."

He slowly sat down again, and I saw by the hesitant look on his face that he didn't want to let me know more about him. But I wasn't going to be the only one in this who had been laid bare.

"I don't want to pry, Alex. That's not what this is about. But you can't deny that you know an awful lot about me, and I know next to nothing about you."

He took a deep breath and slowly exhaled before nodding just once. "Okay. What would you like to know?"

I'd wanted to know the answer to one question since meeting him, so I asked. "Why did you retire from the Baltimore police so young and then move here to Sunset Ridge, of all places?"

"That's a lot for one question," he said, avoiding answering.

"I have more," I said with a smile. "I just thought I'd start with the obvious one. You're very young to be retired from anything."

A frown settled into his features that made me momentarily regret saying anything, and when he spoke I knew that he'd been the Alexander I'd read about in that woman's obituary.

"I left the force after my wife died, and for a while I stayed in the house we'd found together. I thought I could live there, but that wasn't the case. So I moved away from everything that reminded me of that life and bought a house here."

The way he said it told me he was trying to be matter of fact about how much it hurt to lose his wife and leave the life they'd made together in Baltimore, but the sadness in his eyes showed me how much he still remained outside the land of the living.

"Well, I guess we better go then."

"No more questions about the kind of man your new

partner is?" he asked as a look of relief washed over him.

I stood from the table and tossed both of our coffee cups away in the trash. "Nope. Thank you for being willing to answer any. I appreciate that, Alex."

"I have one for you, actually. That picture in your kitchen, the one of Ireland, if I'm not mistaken. Did you take that yourself?"

"No. I wish, but as much as I say I'm going to take a trip there, I've never gone."

He smiled as I set our plates on the counter for Jennie. "So you've got the wanderlust, huh? See? You're nothing like the people here."

"I guess it seems pretty pathetic spending all my time dreaming about places I'll probably never get to, right?"

Alex shook his head. "Dreaming of something more is never pathetic, in my opinion. Take it from me. When you stop dreaming, you stop living."

I didn't know a whole lot about my new partner, but I knew enough to believe that no matter how dark things had been for him, he never stopped dreaming, no matter what he thought.

Chapter Ten

THE SUNSET RIDGE Decorating Committee met every third Tuesday at seven PM in the back room of McGuire's Bar, despite the fact that none of the members ever frequented the bar at any other time of the month. They filed in the front door one by one, each woman clutching a binder with their information on that month's meeting agenda, and walked past the bar without even as much as a hello to my father.

This happened every third Tuesday night of each month like clockwork, and over time, my father had learned to accept the fact that the four ladies weren't so much being rude when they didn't speak to the owner of the building where they met as being what they considered to be proper ladies. These women lived in some kind of time warp where polite women of society didn't go to bars.

Alex and I sat at a table against the far wall away from the front door and watched them walk in and go directly to the back room, eyes straight ahead and chins raised. Standing next to us, my father saw the confusion on Alex's face just as I did and attempted to explain.

"They never speak. Never even say hello when they come for their meetings."

"That seems a bit rude, doesn't it?" Alex asked.

My father looked over at me and smiled. "I'll let Poppy tell you about them while I get your scotch."

As he walked away, I nodded. "It's not so much rude as just who they are."

A look of judgment came over him. "You know you're making my point from lunch."

"I guess, but I don't like thinking that they look down on my father," I said as defensiveness pinched at me. "For the life of me, I can't figure out why they decided to meet here in the first place."

Just then, my father returned with Alex's drink and answered my thought with the story of how the Sunset Ridge Decorating Committee with its four prim and proper ladies chose McGuire's Bar for their meetings.

"It began back when Jefferson Girard was first in the mayor's office. He came to me and asked if his wife's club could meet in my back room once a month. It seemed like he was just trying to help them with a place that would be open when they needed it. I figured it was the neighborly thing to do, and when the newly elected mayor asks you for a favor, you say yes. I quickly realized that he chose my bar here because he would be attending every meeting and Jefferson Girard does love a good glass of whisky."

I watched as the former mayor entered through the same door his wife and her fellow committee members had a few minutes earlier and sat at the edge of the bar where he could clearly see into the back room.

"Dad, I don't think you've ever told me why Mayor Girard accompanies his wife for every meeting."

My father got a sly look on his face and snorted. "I never did find out why, even though he's pretty talkative when he's drinking, but I think he worried that she might do something that would hurt him politically. Now he just comes out of habit."

Alex perked up at my father's answer and asked, "Something that would hurt him politically? Like what? Any idea?"

"I'm not sure. Poppy can tell you that she's more than happy to give her opinion whenever and wherever she can."

I finished his incomplete statement. "Whether it's been asked for or not."

My father smiled. "She also has some quirks. I guess you'd call them idiosyncrasies."

"Like expecting to be called First Lady still, even though her husband is no longer the mayor," I explained.

Alex stifled a laugh and looked over toward the back room where the ladies had assembled. "Really? That's odd."

Leaning down toward us so he could whisper, my father added, "A long time ago, back when you were a little girl, Poppy, I remember it was rumored that she had a drinking problem too."

"Then this is a strange place for her husband to want her to come once a month, isn't it, Dad?"

He shrugged, as if he'd asked himself that question before and never found an answer that satisfied him.

Alex seemed to be enjoying our little gossip session and said, "Perhaps it's the perfect place for her husband."

"He certainly does enjoy those four or five he has every third Tuesday. And the ones he has every Thursday night when he comes in," my father said.

"Four or five drinks in an hour?" Alex asked with curiosity. "That sounds like a lot."

"You know, I've never noticed that but now that you mention it, he does drink quite a bit in the time he's here. I better get back up there and not keep him waiting."

My father left, and I tapped on Alex's arm. "I think I know how you're so good at seeing these people for what they are. You're getting to see them with fresh eyes, while we've been around them almost our entire lives."

"I'd like to think it's more than that," he teased before taking a sip of his drink. "Maybe I'm just an excellent student of human nature."

"I don't doubt it, but I think the fact that you are watching them for something as opposed to us just seeing them all these years helps."

He nodded but said nothing in return, instead taking a few more sips of his scotch before he asked, "How well do you know the women on this committee? They look like they're not your common Sunset Ridge citizens, sort of like our victim. They certainly aren't like Shelley."

"Oh, they aren't. They definitely consider themselves in the upper class of our little town's society, but even so, they aren't of Geneva's station. I met with them the other day for a piece I have to write for *The Eagle*, and they had some very interesting things to say about her."

"Not exactly her biggest fans?"

"You could say that."

"I'm intrigued. What exactly did they say?" he asked, leaning forward toward me so he could hear me when I whispered all they'd told me.

"I think it would be better coming straight from the

horses' mouths, don't you think?" I asked as I stood from the table. "Grab your drink and follow me."

I walked toward the bar and sat down on the side directly in front of the back room entranceway. Alex followed and sat on a barstool next to me. The mayor was far enough away that if we kept our voices low, we might be able to discuss the case, but in truth, I had a feeling we'd be doing more listening than talking. Unless the four ladies of the decorating committee had drastically changed who they fundamentally were, they'd give us an earful about Geneva Woodward.

He leaned in next to me and said quietly, "Do you think they'll just start talking about her without anyone asking a thing?"

I turned and saw the skepticism in his eyes. "I'm betting on it."

Mrs. Girard opened her black binder and read the minutes of the last meeting as the other three women listened to their own words intently, like even a second time they loved hearing what they'd discussed. The First Lady stressed the importance of their idea to purchase new red, white, and blue bunting for the Founders' Day celebration and patriotic holidays coming up in just a few months. The other three nodded their heads in agreement as they no doubt had the month before and then the reading of the minutes ended.

"They really do take this committee seriously, don't they?" Alex said in a low voice next to me.

"I'm sure Mrs. Scanlon has memorized the Parliamentary Procedure handbook."

He craned his neck to see the women and asked, "Which one is she?"

I looked over toward the former mayor to make sure

he didn't know we were watching the ladies, but his attention was on the glass of alcohol in his hand and the basketball game on the television in front of him.

Looking back toward the committee meeting, I gave him the rundown on each of the women. "The lady with the grey hair and the face that looks like she's worked every day of her life is the chairwoman of the decorating committee, Mrs. Scanlon. Regardless of what her face is telling you, she's never worked as long as I've been alive."

Chuckling, he joked, "Maybe it's the rotten insides of her coming out."

I'd thought that myself more than once. Focusing on the woman next to her, I explained about Arlene Dunn. "The woman with the markerhead look like she's used a hair color three shades too dark is the Widow Dunn."

Turning to see his reaction to me referring to someone like it was the eighteenth century, I saw his eyes narrow to slits.

"The Widow Dunn? Are we Puritans now?"

"I don't know why she wants to be called that, but if you ever speak to her and call her anything but the Widow Dunn, you'll get a lecture on how a woman of her stature who has had to deal with the unfortunate circumstances life has heaped upon her should be expected to be referred to in that very way."

"I'll keep that in mind. She doesn't look like she's even fifty years old. How long has she been a widow?"

"A long time. She married some guy who was more sugar daddy than anything else and since he died when I was just a kid, she's been the Widow Dunn."

Alex took a drink of his scotch and shook his head. "This place is like going back in time."

I continued describing the final two members of the committee so he could know the players. "The older woman with the red hair on the right of the widow is Eleanor Girard, whose husband is sitting over there drinking his second whisky."

"The First Lady?"

"Former," I corrected him. "That's her entire claim to fame."

"I do love an accomplished woman," he said with a sneer in his voice.

I chuckled and moved on to Eileen Matthews. "The last woman is the woman who taught me American Literature in junior year in high school—Miss Eileen Matthews."

"Now there's an old maid. Every cell in her body screams she's going to be single forever," he said in my ear.

I turned to see him grinning at me. "Nice. You're going to fit in here in Sunset Ridge perfectly. Maybe we can call you the Retired Detective Montero."

"Don't get angry. I just call them as I see them."

I felt bad for my fellow single female Eileen and waved his justification away. "Just listen. Now that they've gotten the minutes read and decided what they should talk about on tonight's agenda, it will just be a matter of time before they begin attacking Geneva like a bunch of jackals."

True to form, it didn't take the four women long to move from patting themselves on the back for planning the best Founders' Day celebration ever to carving up the life of our murder victim. Even Alex was surprised at how quickly they set aside their task for the night to savage Geneva's reputation.

"Have you heard they think it was some random man who was trying to rob her?" Eileen Matthews asked. As the only committee member who had any shred of kindness in her, I wasn't surprised she was willing to think Geneva's death wasn't tied up in some sordid mess from her personal life.

Plus she was as naïve as they came, so naturally, she would think in the most innocent terms.

Alex whispered in my ear, "Your old high school teacher there sounds like Derek."

I shushed him to continue to listen to what the ladies had to say about Eileen's question. Eleanor Girard piped up quickly with her answer, and as I suspected, it was full of venom and a complete lack of respect for the dead.

"Poppycock! I stand by my initial statement from when I first heard about that woman's death. Finally, one of the women she wronged by sleeping with her husband got her just revenge and Geneva got her just desserts."

I so wanted to jump down off my barstool and ask why she thought that. Was it because she wanted that to be what happened or did she know something and hadn't come forward to tell Derek yet?

"I know she'll probably talk to you, Poppy, but let her go. People are freest with their opinions when they think they're safe and among friends. Plus, maybe she'll give up a name we haven't heard yet in this case," Alex said, obviously sensing how much I wanted to barge in on their get-together to ask some questions.

He was right. I knew that, but I desperately wanted to try out some of the techniques I'd learned by watching him that day. We listened to the Widow Dunn agree with her while Mrs. Scanlon hung back, likely because she feared at any moment they'd accuse her since even though she denied it, her husband had been named as one of Geneva's supposed lovers more than once.

"Enjoying the show?" a voice slurred next to us. "What's on the television is way more interesting. Trust me."

I turned at the same time as Alex to see Jefferson Girard, the former mayor of Sunset Ridge, watching us spy on his wife and her decorating committee friends. Sure he knew what we'd been up to, I quickly flashed him a big smile.

"Hi, Mayor! How are you tonight?"

With his wispy hair that barely covered his head despite his comb-over attempt and jowly face, former mayor Jefferson Girard reminded me of every corrupt politician Hollywood had ever put up on a movie screen. Corpulent in a way that didn't look jolly but always over-indulged, he teetered on his barstool as he downed the last drops of his third whisky for the night.

"I'm fine, Poppy. Just fine. How are you and your friend here?"

"Have you ever met Alex, sir? He's a former detective from Baltimore up here now. Alex, this is the former mayor of Sunset Ridge, Mr. Jefferson Girard."

Alex extended his hand to shake Mr. Girard's. "Alex Montero. It's very nice to meet you, sir."

"Detective? From Baltimore? Did the Hampton brothers bring you up to work on the Geneva Woodward case?" he asked, slurring his words even more.

"No, no. I'm retired from the force for a few years

now. Moved to Sunset Ridge to make a new home for myself. I didn't expect to find a murder up here, though."

Jefferson Girard puffed out his barrel chest and a bit too loudly bragged, "Never on my watch. This town used to be safe. Even the likes of Geneva Woodward didn't have to worry."

Every muscle in my body twitched as his last sentence left his mouth. Even the likes of Geneva Woodward? That didn't sound right. If anything, the politicians in town always kowtowed to people like her, so why was the former mayor slamming her like she was some common streetwalker? A consummate politician, who I'd rarely seen without a smile on his face while he was in office, he never spoke ill of anyone.

Alex gently pushed his forearm against mine to signal me he had picked up on that strange comment too. Waving toward my father at the other end of the bar, he said in Girard's direction, "Let me buy you a drink, sir. Joe, another whisky for the mayor."

I hoped he wouldn't be driving since his bleary, bloodshot eyes already said he'd had enough. Alex obviously wanted to get him and his tongue as loose as possible, and what better way to do it with a hard drinker like Girard than to ply him with more alcohol?

He accepted the glass of whisky and raised it in the air toward the two of us. "To retirement! May yours be as enjoyable as mine has turned out."

We raised our glasses and toasted his retirement, all the while I sat there wishing Alex would get to asking him questions before the decorating committee broke up or Girard got stone drunk and couldn't give a coherent answer. My partner sensed my eagerness and pushed his forearm against mine once again, but a minute or so later, he began feeling the mayor out on what he thought of Geneva.

"It must be quite a shock to everyone around here to have a murder occur. Back in Baltimore, it happened all the time. Too often, unfortunately. But here in Sunset Ridge, it's got to be rare."

The former mayor nodded solemnly and tipped his glass for a gulp of whisky. "It is. Things like that just don't happen in small towns like ours, do they, Poppy?"

"No, sir. And certainly not to people like Geneva Woodward," I said, knowing I was probably rushing things along a bit faster than Alex preferred but by the way Jefferson Girard was beginning to sway on his barstool, I wasn't sure we had much time left to get any real answers out of him.

He snorted in derision at my mention of Geneva and twisted his doughy face into a look of disgust. "People like Geneva. She was nothing more than anyone else in this town. Less than some, I'd say."

"As mayor, you must have known her since I'm sure you knew everyone in town," Alex said in a voice similar to the one he'd used on Shelley earlier that day.

Girard took a mouthful of his drink and banged the glass down onto the bar. "Oh, I knew her. I knew her all too well. Her type is always right there from the minute you come into office. You want to serve the public. You want to make your town better, but her type never wants to help. They could. They have more than enough. But they don't. All they want to do is complain."

I couldn't imagine what Alex could say to that to get him to open up even more. He clearly had a problem with her, but why? I'd never heard anything about a feud between them.

"Running for office and leading a town like this is hard, I imagine," Alex said. "Everybody wants their own way, and a leader has to make tough decisions."

Girard's eyes opened wide, and he nodded. "Yes! It's not as easy as everyone thinks. And despite what some may think, no one is better than anyone else, even if they do have money."

I felt Alex's body tense up next to me and knew the next question would be far more pointed.

"They say she was killed in the middle of the night. I'm thinking most people in town are asleep by that time, so it might be hard for the police to find witnesses. Did you happen to be awake to see anything? I imagine you live in that same section of town, you being such an important person in Sunset Ridge."

The former mayor's temper flared, and he angrily pointed his finger, stabbing it toward us. "Are you accusing me of something, son? How dare you! I'm the mayor of this town!"

Alex tried to smooth his ruffled feathers, but Jefferson Girard slid off his barstool to stand, his finger still pointed directly in our direction. "I was home with my wife all night, as I am every night," he slurred as he took a step toward us. "You're not even a cop in this town, so I don't have to say another word to you."

We sat there stunned at how angry he'd turned so quickly, but before he could say anything else, his wife ran out of the back room clutching her purse and her binder and grabbed a hold of him. She ushered him out of the bar as the other three women followed like ducklings in a row behind her.

"I guess the monthly meeting of the Sunset Ridge

Decorating Committee is over," my father said with a chuckle as he cleared off the bar where Jefferson Girard had sat.

Elbowing Alex, who sat silently finishing his drink, I teased him. "Maybe you should stick to talking to female suspects, and I can talk to the male ones since you had much better luck with Shelley."

He couldn't help but smile at my jab and nodded. "Fair enough, but you have to admit the former mayor sounds like he had a real problem with Geneva."

Excited to hear he and I were on the same track with Girard, I asked, "So are we thinking the former mayor is a suspect?"

He took a sip of his drink and let the scotch sit in his mouth before swallowing. "Yep. We have our second suspect."

"Great! And here I thought all we might get was some dirt on Geneva's life from the committee ladies that could point us to whoever was visiting her for those midnight rendezvous. But isn't Girard our third suspect? You're forgetting the mystery man."

"Maybe," he said with a shrug. "Maybe not."

Chapter Eleven

A FTER THE EXCITEMENT at the bar the night before, I awoke eager to get to work searching for clues about both of our known suspects and their relationships to Geneva. I doubted Shelley was ever as close to our victim as she claimed, and Jefferson Girard's outburst at the mere mention of Geneva was definitely interesting, to say the least.

Rolling over in bed, I looked over at the night table and saw my phone blinking. Someone had texted me. Quickly, I swiped the screen to see who had contacted me, happy that it was unlikely my father since he'd never used a phone for that reason in his life. Joe McGuire was nothing if not old school.

Highlighted was a message from a number I didn't recognize. I opened it and saw an invitation.

Meet me at The Grounds at 9.

Confused as to who had sent it, I messaged back.

Who is this?

Seconds later, another text came in.

Alex.

Alex? I didn't remember giving him my number. True, I should have since we were working together on this case, but I hadn't, so how had he gotten it? It wasn't like cell phone numbers were listed in the phone book.

Curious, I typed out yet another question.

How did you get my number?

Again, just seconds later, he texted back.

Detective. Remember?

I couldn't help but smile. For all that seriousness he often showed, he could be quite funny. Texting back, I asked my question again.

Enough with the detective thing. Really how did you get it?

As I waited for his answer, I tried to figure out when he could have gotten my number. Had he lifted my phone out of my purse at some point? Funny and cute was one thing, but invading my person was something entirely different. If he had done that, Alex Montero was about to find out how unkind and how like the rest of Sunset Ridge's residents I could be.

But then he messaged back, and I couldn't be mad at him.

I saw your number on Derek's desk when I went to see him yesterday. So have you interrogated me enough to meet at The Grounds at 9?

Okay, so he wasn't a pickpocket. Good. Looking at

the time, I saw it was already after eight and I remembered I had to be at *The Eagle* before noon to get some work done on my weekly article.

Okay, but I might be a little late. I'll be there, though.

Tossing my phone on the bed, I hurried to the shower without even having my first cup of morning coffee. Such was the punishment for oversleeping.

ALEX WAITED FOR me with a coffee and a cherry danish at the same table we'd sat at yesterday. The Grounds was nowhere near as crowded this morning, although I was far later making my first appearance of the day.

Jennie waved at me as I walked toward the back of the shop and said in a low voice as I passed, "Are you and that guy together, Poppy? He is one sweet catch."

I'd never heard her speak about anyone like that since we weren't exactly friends. Surprised at her comment about Alex, I simply smiled and shook my head. "No. We're not like that. Just friends."

Twirling her blond hair around her finger, she looked back at him as he sat waiting and then looked back toward me. "You're missing a fine opportunity, hun. If you don't move quick, somebody's going to snatch him up and then you'll be stuck in the friend zone."

I had to roll my eyes at the friend zone comment. Whatever zone Alex and I were in, I was happy with where we stood.

"Thanks, Jennie. I'll talk to you later."

She accepted my noncommittal brush off, but as I

walked away I heard her say, "I wouldn't be ignoring that if I had the chance."

I reached the table and sat down across Alex, who sat there with his arms crossed studying the rest of the coffee shop customers. "Sorry I took so long."

"No problem. It gave me time to do some people watching. Interesting stuff. By the way, I thought you handled the waitress pretty well."

Taking a sip of my coffee, I saw what looked like a twinkle in his eye. "You're all the rage here in town, it seems. Did you see the way the ladies looked at us as they were leaving the bar last night? I could almost read their minds. They wanted to know if we were together."

A slow grin spread across his mouth, and his eyes twinkled a little brighter. "Oh well. Nothing like being consigned to Poppy McGuire's friend zone."

"Can we get down to business and leave the silliness to the rest of Sunset Ridge's residents? I can't tell you how much it means to me to know someone who doesn't get involved in the nonsense. I'd hate to have you disappointment me and become like everyone else here."

He took a drink of his coffee and said, "I'll do my best. So you've had a few hours to think of our two suspects. Any ideas?"

I thought for a moment, but it was too early for me to be doing any real detective work. "I haven't even had a first cup of coffee yet, Alex. How about you take the lead this morning?"

"Okay. So far we have two people who in varying degrees seem to have had a problem with our victim. Shelley Steadman, the new money on the block, acts like she and Geneva were the best of friends, but do we have any proof of that?"

I thought about never seeing the two of them together and shook my head. "None at all. I've seen Geneva Woodward go to Diamanti's a few times a week for years and never once have I seen her with anyone, including Shelley. It seems odd to me that if they were so close that they wouldn't at least eat dinner together once in a while."

Alex agreed. "So she likely lied about how close she and Geneva were."

"Or really thought they were that close and suddenly that night found out they weren't," I added.

"Very good. That coffee must be kicking in."

Pleased with my ability to see something he considered valuable, I continued on with what might have happened that night between Shelley and Geneva. "Okay, so assuming she found out that the person she desperately wanted to be like didn't much like her, did she become enraged and strangle Geneva? She did almost let it slip that she wanted to call her a bitch when I talked to her."

"Maybe. I'm not convinced Shelley is our killer, though."

I watched as he folded his arms across his chest again. To be honest, I didn't feel very strongly about Shelley as the killer either.

"She would have had a hard time committing the crime if she can't even carry a tray with iced tea and cookies," I wondered aloud. "What did she say she had a problem with?"

Alex reached into his coat and took out a small notepad like the one I used for my job at *The Eagle*. Flipping through the pages, he stopped after four or five and said, "She said she couldn't lift anything heavy because of all the years she'd worked."

Curious how he had noted that detail since I didn't see him write anything down while we were speaking to Shelley, I asked, "How did you remember that? You never take notes while we're together."

He looked up from his notebook and explained, "I have a pretty good memory, but I write down everything important from each day when I get home at night."

"Really?" I asked in disbelief. I guess I had thought he just remembered all these details and didn't have to use notes like I had to.

"Sure," he said with a smile. "Even I can't recall everything people say days later without some kind of help."

He flipped through a few more pages as I wondered if maybe I had the stuff to make a good detective. Maybe all I needed was some experience.

"What about the former mayor?" I asked. "What kind of notes do you have on him?"

"Oh, his notes could take up this whole tablet. He's an interesting guy, that former mayor. I think we can safely say at the very least that he's a heavy drinker and he's got a temper on him."

"Considering we watched him put down five drinks in the span of just over an hour, yes, I'd say we can call him a heavy drinker. You know, I've seen him in the bar week after week for years, and I'd never noticed he drank as much as he did last night. He seemed in rare form."

Alex arched one dark eyebrow as a curious look crossed his face. "Maybe he's drinking to forget something?"

"I don't know, but he was definitely putting them

away last night more than even my father had ever seen him do."

Alex smiled. "Guilty conscience?"

"Could be. I want to do some research on him today after I get done at work."

"Good idea. I did some last night after I got home. Former mayor Girard's record is pretty clean. He was well-liked by the voters until this last year, but I couldn't find out why they sent him out of office after twelve years."

Everyone who was around for last year's election season could tell Alex about what had cost the mayor his job. It was all anyone could talk about all fall. Although in the big picture it hadn't really meant much, to the local people in Sunset Ridge a once beloved mayor losing re-election was big news.

"Let's just say that he butt heads with the wrong person and came out on the losing side of the battle."

Leaning back in his seat, Alex looked across the table at me with a quizzical expression. "Really? Anyone I'd know?"

I nodded. "Our very own police chief, Dominick Hampton himself. Seems the mayor thought himself above the law one too many times and the chief wasn't having it. So he let it be known that Jefferson Girard wasn't the man he seemed to be."

"Let me guess. Was he caught drinking and driving?"

"You'd think that, but no. Nothing like that. The mayor was caught fudging his property taxes. The poor lady in the town tax office, Annabelle Jarvis, who had been helping him skimp on paying lost her job and moved away from Sunset Ridge a week later. Now if

Girard had been found murdered, she'd be the person I'd be looking at for that. She swore he forced her to go along with his cheating scheme, but nobody wanted to hear about it. So they shunned her and sent him from the mayor's office."

Alex knitted his brows in what looked like confusion. "There were nearly a dozen people other than us and Girard in the bar last night, and every person who saw him said hi and gave him a big smile as they did it. If they had such a problem with his behavior, it doesn't seem like it's still an issue."

I had to smile at his big city naiveté, if there was such a thing. Coming from a place like Baltimore, he seemed more used to the directness of city people. Small towns weren't like that. Oh, the citizens of Sunset Ridge had made Jefferson Girard pay for his malfeasance and taken his job away, but he was, after all, a man who'd led the town for over a decade, so it wasn't like they were going to hold a grudge forever. He'd paid his price, so now he could live his life.

And people would just whisper behind his back from time to time. That was what small town life was like.

"You have to remember where you are, Alex. This isn't the big city. Things are done differently here. They drove him out of office, but after he publically agreed to pay all his back taxes he owed, everyone pretty much shrugged and went on to the next piece of juicy gossip. You know, like who's unmarried or who's sleeping with whom. It's just the way this place is."

"Interesting."

I took a forkful of my danish and enjoyed the taste of the cherry flavor on my tongue. "You'll get used to it."

"I'm not sure I want to. I prefer a more

straightforward approach to life," Alex said in a voice tinged with disgust.

"That's why you're friends with me. I'm your local connection for straightforward," I said with a smile.

Some part of me didn't want him to think that all my hometown had to offer was nasty old biddies who gossiped too much and corrupt politicians. True, it did have them and I hated how nosy the busybodies could be, but Sunset Ridge was so much more and I wanted him to see that.

"You and our favorite policeman, who I see coming our way with a look of determination, if I'm not mistaken."

I followed Alex's gaze to see Derek walking up to our table indeed with an expression that said he had something on his mind. Dressed in his blue police uniform, he stood out from the rest of The Grounds' customers, all of whom now watched him approach us. Tongues would be wagging that afternoon, for sure.

"I'm glad I found you both here. Mind if I sit down?" Derek asked as he pulled a chair from a nearby table.

"Please do. You seem to have something important to tell us," Alex said as he cleared his coffee cup and plate away from where Derek chose to sit.

"How can you tell?" he asked as he moved his chair close to the table.

Before Alex could answer, I did it for him. "Detective, remember?"

Across the table, Alex gave me a sly grin as Derek looked at me like I'd said something confusing.

"Yeah, well I'm here to ask what you've found out so far since I know the two of you are working on the

Geneva Woodward murder case. Since I just ran into a big, fat dead end, I'm hoping to hear you're having more success."

Feeling particularly vindicated since I'd never believed in his robbery gone bad theory of the case, I asked, "What happened to the thief lead?"

"The state police just called. They searched his place and although he had hundreds of pieces of jewelry, none of them they found matched the inventory Geneva's insurance gave me. According to their records, not one piece is missing and nothing else seems to be missing from her house."

"So you found Geneva's rings in her house?"

Derek thought about my question and shook his head. "No. Now that you bring it up, we didn't."

Looking across the table at Alex, I smiled. "So it wasn't just a murder, after all. Interesting."

"Definitely. Our murderer had something other than murder on their mind."

"Great. I thought I was back to square one but now I'm not even there yet. Please tell me you two found something."

I placed my hand on Derek's and couldn't resist teasing him. "We're so glad you've come over to the dark side. Things are way more interesting over here."

My joking perked him up, and for the first time since he joined us he didn't look like the weight of the world was resting on his shoulders. "Oh yeah? I'm all ears."

Alex smiled at me and began telling him about what we'd found out by talking to Shelley and the former mayor. When he finished, Derek looked at both of us and said, "You two have been busy. I'm definitely interested in speaking to both of them."

"I'm more for Girard, but Alex will probably tell you his mind is still open."

Derek's happiness faded slightly, and his mouth turned down into a tiny frown. "Speaking to the former mayor might be a little difficult. It's never just Jefferson you get to deal with, and once that wife of his gets wind that I might think he's a suspect, it will be all over town. Maybe for now I'll keep things to myself until I can find out anything more."

"Do you really think she'll spread that kind of news?" I asked. "I'd think the First Lady would want to keep that her husband might be a suspect under wraps."

He sighed like most people did when they thought about dealing with either Girard. "Maybe I'm wrong, but regardless, I'll have to treat him with kid gloves. He is the former mayor, you know."

"A former mayor who was cheating on his property taxes," Alex added with another hint of disgust in his tone. "It's not like he hasn't been a part of something illegal before."

Derek seemed confused by Alex's comments, so I patted him on the hand again and explained, "He's not used to how things work around here yet. Give him time."

I saw by the way Alex opened his mouth to speak that he wasn't eager to get used to how Sunset Ridge worked, but before he could say anything else Dominick Hampton showed up and joined us at our table. Never a fan of my amateur investigating, he likely wouldn't be happy at all to find out that I was any part of the Geneva Woodward case, so I braced for the usual snideness he liked to dish out to me whenever he saw me with his brother.

"Derek, a minute of your time, please," he said as he pointed toward the area back near the restrooms. Derek quickly followed his brother there while Alex and I looked at each other like we both knew what the other was thinking. Whatever Dominick had to say, we wanted to hear it.

"Did I just hear you say Jefferson Girard is a suspect in our murder case?" he asked in a low voice barely loud enough for me to make out.

With his back to us, Derek nodded. "Don't worry, Dom. I can handle this with the mayor."

"Former mayor and if he's part of this, he won't be getting any free passes from us. If you have good cause, get him in for questioning."

Alex and I stared across the table at one another but didn't say a thing. Surprised at his brother's eagerness to go after Girard, I tried to push out the noise around us to hear what else Dominick had to say, but I was unsuccessful. All I heard was Derek promise he wouldn't give Jefferson any special treatment.

With that, the chief of police left his brother standing alone, and as he passed us, he tapped his knuckles on our table and smiled down at me. "Poppy. Alex."

Before we could even say hello, he was gone. Obviously Derek had been able to keep my work on the case secret. Good. I didn't need to be chewed out by Dominick another time.

Derek returned to the table and replaced his chair at the table next to us. "I better get going since I have some work to do. If you find out anything else, remember your promise, Poppy."

"I will. Whatever we find out is all yours."

Turning to look at Alex, Derek extended his hand to

shake his. "Good to see you again, Alex. Thanks for your help."

With the second Hampton brother gone, I couldn't wait to discuss with Alex what we'd heard. "What do you think of that?"

"He seems pretty eager to see Jefferson Girard mixed up in this."

What Alex said did sort of make sense. "I guess, but even with that property tax issue, I remember Derek telling me that his brother really didn't want to have everything go public. He only did it after Girard basically told him he could do whatever he wanted because he was the mayor."

"Perhaps he has information that we don't know about? As police chief, he would know about things concerning the mayor's office that the average citizen wouldn't," Alex suggested.

"True, and it is a murder case, so I wouldn't expect the chief to take any possible lead lightly."

Looking down at my watch, I saw it was nearly noon. "I wish I could stay and discuss this, but the social page of *The Eagle* calls. Let me know if you find out anything with our case."

He just nodded and smiled, like he often did, and as I made my way outside to walk to work, I liked the way it sounded when I said our case. We had a case we were working together, and I was actually helping.

Our case. It had a nice ring to it.

Chapter Twelve

MY BOSS WAS nowhere to be found by the time I got to *The Eagle*'s offices, so at least I wouldn't have to explain to him why I'd likely have to meet with the Founders' Day committee one more time to write my series of articles. A man particularly disinterested in anything that even hinted at a mystery, he'd never understand how my interview became derailed with talk of who killed Geneva Woodward or why I was even curious about the case.

I settled in behind my desk and opened the file for the article I had due the next day. A fluff piece about the gardens of the residents of Sunset Ridge, it wasn't exactly going to require much of my writing skills. I received this same assignment every year, and my editor didn't expect anything new in this piece. The first year I got it, I went out to each garden in town and took copious notes as I spoke to each homeowner about what they'd done to achieve such a beautiful display of flowers. I had details on everything from the type and amount of fertilizer each one used to how many hours a day they devoted to tending their gardens.

My boss's reaction? Just make sure there are more pictures than words, Poppy. And stop writing as if this is a topic that requires all those details. Then he threw out a quote from Hamlet about words to let me know all the work I'd done would never show up in the paper before he spun on his heels and left my office in disgust at my diligence.

So now I read over my piece from last year, the year before, and every year since the first time I wrote it and cringed at the mediocrity of each sentence. I wanted to do better. I wanted to write something that would really showcase those gardens, even though I'd grown to hate them for what they represented to me.

I didn't, though. Instead, I did as my editor demanded and only changed a word here and a phrase there, things he wouldn't notice but that let me feel like I wasn't merely his obedient lackey.

"Hey you!"

I spun around at the sound of Bethany's chipper voice and saw her standing in the doorway to my office. Smiling at me, she tilted her head so her blond hair tumbled over to her left shoulder.

"What's new, caribou?"

"Just doing my yearly homage to flowers. You know, the one that Howard uses to make me understand exactly what my place here is."

Bethany stepped into my office and sat down in the chair next to my desk. "Don't let him get you down. Everyone loves your articles. You're the rock star of the paper. You don't see that awful editor of yours or any of those reporters getting stopped on the street like you do when we go for lunch."

I chuckled at her reference to the time we went to eat at The Madison Diner a few months earlier. Something I'd written about the Pumpkin Festival that occurred each October had affected Maria Carson, the owner of Carson's Floral Shop, and she stopped me on the street to rave about how much she'd loved the article.

"Yeah, rock star, baby. I'll have to remember that."

Bethany leaned forward toward me and looked around like she wanted to check if we were alone before she spoke. "So what's the news on Geneva's murder? Got any clues you can tell me about?"

"Nothing yet," I lied, wishing I could tell her more.

She leaned back in her chair and shook her head. "I still can't believe it. So it's you and Derek working together? To be honest, I'm putting my money on you solving this. Nothing against Derek, but I'm just not sure he has what it takes to solve a murder."

"And I do?"

With a giggle, she said, "I'm going with girl power on this one. You're smart, Poppy. You read people like no one I've ever known. If I had your skills, maybe I wouldn't always date the wrong men."

Bethany had a terrible track record with men. If her boyfriends weren't addicted to something, they had pasts that inevitably came back to haunt them just when she was sure she'd found "The One." Her relationships never lasted, but I didn't think the blame lay completely with her. She simply had bad luck picking men.

But since she always had a boyfriend, none of the nosy gossips in town ever seemed to bother whispering about her. In their strange mindset, it was better for a woman to have a string of terrible boyfriends than avoid the messy drama of bad men and have no man at all.

"How is your current man doing? What was his name?"

Shrugging, she twisted her face into a grimace. "I'm single again. Rex turned out to be another bad one."

"Ah, that's right. T-Rex. Now that you're done with him, I can admit that every time I thought about him, all I could think about was a dinosaur flailing his tiny arms."

"That I might have been able to handle, but his two-timing me with that ex-girlfriend of his was a no go."

I touched her arm in sympathy, knowing that even though she sounded okay, it always hurt to be cheated on. "I'm sorry. Is it time for the men suck discussion?"

She rewarded my joke with a big smile. At least I was able to give her that.

"No. There's no need to state the obvious. Maybe it's time for me to just admit that this is how it's supposed to be for me. Or maybe I'm supposed to be a nun."

Now it was my turn to smile, and with a chuckle, I said, "I think the train left that station a long time ago."

"Yeah. Woo-woo! So that's out of the question."

"Where would you find a nunnery these days anyway, right? It's just not a job that's around much anymore," I teased, gaining another giggle from her.

Behind us, someone knocked on my door and we turned to see Jesse the mail boy standing in my doorway with an envelope in his hand. "Here's a letter for you, Poppy."

Jesse had a cute smile and a body that Bethany and I had checked out more than once. A freshman at one of the local colleges, he was only nineteen, so every time we let our gazes run all over his very muscular form, we both chided ourselves for it. Well, I chided myself. Bethany not so much.

Taking the letter from him, I smiled and tried to keep my eyes on his very cute face, but it wasn't possible. As I thanked him, my gaze slid down over his torso straining against his t-shirt, instantly making me feel like I was violating him.

"Nice to see you again. You too, Bethany. I don't have any mail for you, but maybe next time."

I heard Bethany make a tiny moaning sound before she said, "Definitely next time, Jesse."

He moved on to his next mail stop as we giggled like teenage girls. "We're terrible, you know that?"

Bethany shook her head and pressed her lips together like she was in pain. "What's terrible is that he's so young. If he was just five years older, I'd be all over that like white on rice."

"Well, that would be only a four year difference for you. It would still be too young for me, though."

"If only. As it is, he's just too young. But that won't stop me from looking."

As she sat fantasizing about *The Eagle*'s mail boy, I opened my envelope and began reading my letter. It didn't take long for me to realize this wasn't just another letter from a reader.

It's a shame about Geneva Woodward being murdered. A good lead could be to talk to Candy Skerrit since she had as much reason to hate her as anyone in town. Maybe even more.

I looked to the bottom of the page and saw no signature. I turned the envelope over to see there was no return address either. An anonymous message about a potential suspect? I'd have to tell Alex about this as soon as Bethany left.

My cell phone rang just as I looked at the plain white sheet of paper, and I saw it was my partner calling me.

Answering it, I asked, "Reading my mind now?"

"What?" he asked in return, clearly confused by how I'd begun our conversation.

"Nothing. I'll tell you later. What's up?"

"What do you think about dinner at Diamanti's tonight?"

His question floored me, and for a moment, I didn't know what to say. When my brain finally turned back on, I stammered, "I…I…okay. Sure, okay."

"I'll pick you up at seven. See you then."

Pulling the phone away from my ear, I looked at it like it was some kind of foreign object I couldn't figure out as Alex ended the call. Dinner at Diamanti's? What was that about?

"Poppy, what's up? Is something wrong?"

I turned to look at Bethany and saw by the worried look on her face that I must have seemed shaken up by Alex's call. Forcing myself back to normal, I waved off her concern and pretended everything was good.

"It's nothing. Just a little surprised is all."

"Who was that? Is something going on with your father?"

I set my phone down on my desk. My father? Why would she ask that? Then I realized she'd likely jump to that conclusion since he was the only person I ever worried about.

"No, it wasn't my father. That call was from Alex."

Bethany practically jumped out of her chair. "Alex? Who's Alex? Are you with a guy now, Poppy?"

"No, no. He's the retired detective from Baltimore

who moved here a while ago and offered to work with me to investigate Geneva's murder. Remember me telling you about him? He turned out to be a decent guy, even though we had a rough few meetings in the beginning."

Her blue eyes opened wide and her mouth fell open. "Oh my God! I heard about him from Jennie when I got my coffee yesterday. She told me he's hot! And you're working with him on this case?"

Rolling my eyes at Jennie's description of Alex, I nodded. "Yeah. He's teaching me a lot. I'm so impressed by how good a detective he is."

"I don't care about that. Is he hot like Jennie said?"

I thought about her question for a moment. Was he good looking like Jennie thought? Alex definitely had a nice look about him, and those brown eyes were definitely the kind a woman could get lost in. And he did have a great body. Oh my God! What was I thinking? Alex was a friend and colleague, and that was it.

"Well? Poppy, are you going to answer me?" Bethany pressed with a nudge to my arm.

Shaking my thoughts out of my head, I said, "Sorry. I was thinking about something else. I guess Alex could be considered attractive. I don't really notice that about him, though. I'm more interested in his abilities as a detective."

So that wasn't exactly the truth. It didn't matter anyway. I admired Alex for his investigative skills more than anything else. That's what mattered.

"What did he say that shook you up like that?"

"He asked me to go to dinner at Diamanti's tonight."

Bethany cooed, "Well, you may not think of him any

way other than professionally, but he obviously thinks that of you. What are you going to do?"

Confused, I looked at her unsure what she meant. "What do you mean? I'm going to dinner, of course."

"I mean about dating him."

I dismissed her idea immediately. "I'm not dating him, and he doesn't want to date me, Bethany. I'm sure this is about the case."

Leveling a disapproving stare at me, she waved away my suggestion that dinner was nothing more than two colleagues getting together to talk about their work. "I'm sure you're wrong. If he just wanted to talk about the case, he wouldn't have asked you to dinner at the finest restaurant in town. So you need to start seeing this for what it is."

While I didn't want to disagree with her, I didn't think this was a date. I wasn't sure what it was, but it couldn't be a date. It couldn't be, could it? What if she was right?

"Well, whatever it is, I have work to do," I said in an attempt to give Bethany the clue I needed her to leave so I could go talk to Candy Skerrit before it was time to meet Alex.

"What are you going to wear? Do you have a little black dress? I think that would look great. And you can do your hair in an upsweep look that would be terrific." She stood to leave and added, "I expect to hear all the juicy details tomorrow, Poppy. If you don't come in to work, you better call me."

"There will be no details, so don't expect anything."

"I've known you for over three years and never once have I seen your eyes sparkle at a mere dinner meeting, so I'm expecting this to go well. I'll talk to you tomorrow, but have a good time tonight."

She gave my shoulder a tiny squeeze as she left, and I was glad to not have to protest again that this wasn't a date because the more she talked about it, the more I had to admit I really wasn't sure what this was.

Or how I felt about it.

Maybe her idea of the upswept look was good, though, and what better place to get that done than Candy Skerrit's beauty shop, Candy's Cuts? Hopefully, I could get Candy to fit me into her schedule, and while I got my hair done for dinner, I could ask her some questions.

Pleased with myself for coming up with an idea that would kill two birds with one stone, I closed my laptop and headed over to Candy's beauty shop on the opposite end of town.

CANDY'S CUTS LOOKED like nothing special on the outside, even though it was the most popular beauty shop in town. The storefront windows merely had the name of the business in black letters and the building the shop was in was an old rundown brick type popular in Sunset Ridge.

The outside of its owner was similarly plain. Nothing special to look at with straight brown hair that hung in no particular style at all down to her shoulders and a face that rarely had any makeup on it, Candy Skerrit was also a woman with a streak of honesty that usually showed itself as rudeness. If she didn't like you, then you could expect her to spew her opinions on everything about your appearance, whether you asked for them or not. I'd never been on the receiving end of her rudeness, but I'd seen it in person more than once at her shop.

I opened the door and walked in to see three women in various stages of having their hair done. Two sat under dryers and one sat in Candy's chair as she snipped away at the layers in the woman's hair. I didn't see her assistant Kira anywhere in the shop, so I cautiously approached where Candy worked. Self-consciously fingering the bottom of my light brown hair, I hoped I wouldn't be the latest victim of her brand of honesty.

"Poppy McGuire, what are you doing here? Do you have an appointment?" she asked as she looked at me in the mirror.

"No, but I was hoping that you might be able to squeeze me in."

I saw the woman sitting in the chair getting her hair done look into the mirror with terror in her eyes. Candy frowned, but I didn't get the response her customer feared.

"I guess I can probably squeeze you in. What are you looking for?"

Looking down at the split ends at the bottom of my hair, I cringed. "Just a trim and maybe if you could do my hair in an upsweep do?"

Candy's oddly unkempt eyebrows shot up. "Really? Have somewhere special to go?"

"No, just wanted to try something new," I said in my most casual voice and hoped she hadn't heard Jennie's gossip about my partner.

"Okay, I think I can do that. Just give me a few so I can get these three done."

I took a seat near the two women under the dryers and waited about a half hour before she was free. When everyone else had left and she'd returned from smoking a cigarette outside, Candy waved me toward her chair.

"So how have you been, Poppy? Still working at the newspaper?" she asked as she wrapped a black cape around my shoulders to catch the hair she cut.

"I am."

"Does anyone read the newspaper anymore? I read all my news on the computer."

"You know how the people in this town are. They're set in their ways, so *The Eagle* gets to benefit from that."

She gave me a knowing smile in the mirror and turned me around to wash my hair. "I definitely do know this town. Having lived here for all my life, I know these people live in a time warp. Do you know that when I divorced Mr. Skerrit the old ladies in town couldn't wait to ask me how I was going to find another husband?"

As she lowered me back toward the sink, I said, "I just ignore them. It's not like there's a guy in this town I'm interested in anyway."

She washed my hair and made small talk about how much she hated the busybodies in town. Every so often, I nodded to keep the conversation going, but I really wanted to seize a chance to introduce Geneva's murder into it to see if the anonymous letter writer was correct.

Lifting the chair, she turned me toward the mirror and began cutting the bottom of my hair before I even told her how much I wanted trimmed off. I knew better than to stop her, though, unless I wanted an earful of her kind of truth, so I left my look in her hands and hoped for the best.

Ten minutes and about an inch later, she was done cutting my hair and had dried it enough to begin working her magic to give me the upswept look Bethany had suggested. As she twisted and pinned my hair into the most romantic style I'd ever worn, it suddenly became a possibility in my mind that the dinner I'd have with Alex in just a few hours could be a date.

I needed to get that ridiculous notion out of my head, so while Candy concentrated on giving me what she called "the sexy look," I took a chance that she might be willing to let me chat her up about Geneva.

In my smoothest voice, I said, "So how about what happened to Geneva Woodward right here in Sunset Ridge?"

Candy's fingers stopped their movement at the back of my head, and I averted my eyes from the mirror just in case my motives were obvious in them. She didn't say anything for a moment, and when she finally spoke, I knew the person who'd anonymously sent me that letter hadn't lied.

At least not about Candy hating Geneva.

"That woman! Nothing was ever good enough for her. She'd come in for a color and cut, and it never failed. She was always dissatisfied. I swear to God I was tempted this last time to tell her to never come back again!"

She jabbed my scalp with a hairpin and quickly apologized, but if a little beauty tragedy was the cost to get information out of her that may help Alex and me solve the case, then that was a price I was willing to pay.

Waving off the stab and the real pain radiating across the top of my head, I pushed on. "I've heard from others around town that she could be difficult at times."

"Difficult?" Candy snapped. "I can tell you stories that would make you see me as a saint compared to her. I did exactly what she wanted every time she came in here, and each time she stiffed me with no tip. She's lucky I never turned her hair bright blue. I'm surprised she was able to ever get Girard to give her a second look with how nasty she was."

"She certainly had a way of angering people," I said into the mirror as I watched for Candy's reaction, but then what she'd said about the former mayor hit me light a bolt of lightning. "Was he cheating on his wife with her?"

"I think so. At least once a week I'd see the two of them a block or so away near the park talking like they were meeting in secret." Her eyes flashed true rage, and she returned to her own issues with Geneva. "Every one of my customers had to pay for that woman's cheapskate ways!"

I opened my mouth to ask her if she knew anything more about Geneva and Mayor Girard, but her assistant Kira interrupted us to let her know her next appointment had arrived. Candy apologized and left me in the chair right after she finished my upsweep, and I was sure I'd missed my opportunity to get any real details about the affair or her feud with Geneva.

As I sat there admiring her work on my hair, Kira sat down in the chair next to me and leaned over to ask, "Did I hear you talking about Geneva Woodward? I'm not surprised someone murdered her. She was a miserly woman. All that money and she refused to tip Candy whenever she did her hair."

"I guess there was no love lost between them?"

Kira shook her head and whispered, "No, and Candy was fed up with her. I heard her say she was going to get revenge on her someday soon for being so nasty and never tipping her. After that last time, I was worried they'd get into a fight right here in the shop."

"Really? It was that bad?"

"Yeah. Geneva called her a ham-handed, second-rate barber and threw her fifty dollars on my desk before storming out. I thought Candy would wring her neck. She chased after her out onto the sidewalk, but Geneva got into her car and drove away too quickly."

"That sounds pretty bad. She really did know how to make enemies."

I saw Candy coming toward us in the mirror, and before I could get anything more out of Kira, she quickly ran to the front of the shop. I'd gotten some good information out of her about how much Candy hated Geneva, and maybe I'd found another suspect.

Tucking a few stray hairs into my hairdo, she smiled at me in the mirror. "Looks terrific! I like this look on your, Poppy. It's way sexier than your usual boring look with your hair just hanging straight and doing nothing in particular."

There was that classic Candy truthfulness that stung with each word. That she could dish it out was certain, but maybe she couldn't take it in return. Perhaps words weren't enough to get revenge on Geneva for her brand of truthfulness, and she'd taken it to a higher level that night.

Chapter Thirteen

B Y QUARTER TO seven, I stood in my kitchen dressed and ready for whatever Alex and I were going to do at Diamanti's. Well, whatever we were going to do other than eat. As Bethany had suggested, I wore my sleeveless little black dress with my favorite black pumps, and together with my fancy hairdo and makeup done up to accentuate my eyes and lips as all the magazines suggested, my look was just as Candy had said.

Way sexier. Whether it was appropriate for our dinner was an entirely different story.

At exactly seven o'clock, Alex knocked on my door. I opened it to see him like I'd never seen him look before. He wore a dark grey suit, a black dress shirt, and a red and grey tie. For the first time, I thought I saw what Jennie saw.

Dressed like this, I couldn't deny it. Alex was hot. Actually, it was more than that. He was stunning, like the kind of good looking I'd never seen in Sunset Ridge. Lost in thought about how gorgeous he looked, I said nothing and simply stared at him as I held the door open.

"Is something wrong?" he asked, shaking me from my thoughts.

"No. Please come in," I answered as I gathered my composure.

Alex looked around my kitchen as if he was searching for a reason why I was acting so weird, and when he couldn't find one, he said, "I'm looking forward to this dinner at Diamanti's. In all the time I've lived here, I've never gone there."

"It's very nice. Great food. I've always enjoyed it."

I didn't know why I was speaking in staccato, explaining things like people did in their reviews on travel sites. I'd been to Diamanti's countless times, and the food had never disappointed. Why I didn't tell him that I didn't know, but if I didn't stop acting like a teenage girl on her first real date, we'd never have a chance to have a good time.

At whatever we were doing.

"Are you ready? Should we go?"

I reached for my bag and uncomfortably said, "Sure. I'm fine. I mean ready to go. Let's go."

God, I really was acting like a teenage girl.

Snap out of it, Poppy! You've been on dates hundreds of times, and this probably isn't even a date. Just two co-workers getting together to talk about something they're working on. See? There's no reason to be acting so awkwardly. Get it together!

Alex guided me out of my kitchen and closed the door behind us. We silently walked out toward the sidewalk, but instead of turning toward downtown, he gently took hold of my arm to steer me the opposite way.

"My car is parked up here a little ways."

Surprised we were driving, I asked, "We're not walking to the restaurant?" My house wasn't even six blocks away from Diamanti's, so I'd assumed we would walk.

His gaze drifted from my face down my body to my high heels and then back up to my eyes. "In those shoes? I would never expect anyone to walk in heels that high."

Self-conscious about my choice of footwear for the night, I began explaining how they were the right shoes for the outfit and how I'd worn them before so I knew I could handle walking even a few blocks in them. To be honest, I knew I was rambling and wanted to stop myself, but somehow I was unable to.

Alex smiled and extended his arm toward his Mustang. "They look great, Poppy. I just don't feel right having you walk all that way. Humor me, okay?"

I sighed. "Okay. Thanks."

Whatever this night was, it wasn't starting off well. Not for me, at least. For his part, Alex seemed perfectly relaxed in comparison to my one woman show about how uncomfortable I was in my own skin. Not five minutes after he picked me up and I already felt foolish.

Definitely not a good start.

We drove the few blocks to Diamanti's and didn't say a word. For once, I was thankful for his ability to be silent. At least that decreased the chances of my sticking my foot in my mouth again. Normally, I would have chatted about his car since I hadn't asked him anything about it yet, but I didn't want to risk sounding like an idiot on that topic too.

By the time we reached the restaurant, I'd convinced myself that I was acting silly. This was Alex, after all. My partner. My friend, or at least someone who was quickly becoming a friend. And no matter what Jennie or others in town thought of him, he was just the person I worked with for this case.

The maître d' sat us at a table in the center of the

restaurant on Alex's request. From behind the menu, I wondered why he'd specifically asked to be seated in that particular spot, but I didn't ask. He liked to people watch, so perhaps that was the reason.

That would also point to the idea that this wasn't, in fact, a date but something related to our investigation of the case. Although I couldn't help be disappointed at that for a brief moment, the thought of this just being us working together as partners, albeit dressed to the teeth and eating at a fine restaurant, relaxed me.

"If you love a great steak, this is the right place for it," I said, breaking the silence between us.

Alex peered out from behind his menu and smiled. "I could go for a good steak tonight. What about you?"

Looking down the menu, I saw my favorite Diamanti's dish. "I think I'm going for the bourbon pork chop."

"Sounds good."

We made small talk about what sides to get, and I told him about how I'd always found the bartenders there to be a little too heavy handed with the alcohol in the martinis. Then we ordered our food and drinks. For the first time that night, I didn't feel like I was unsure of myself. I pushed the last of Bethany's silliness about what this was out of my head and just let myself have a good time with someone I admired.

And once I'd done that, we were able to get back to business about Geneva's murder and the person who was very possibly our newest suspect.

Reaching into my bag, I pulled out the letter I'd received at my office earlier that day. "I have something to show you. It was delivered to me at *The Eagle* while I was at work today."

I handed it to Alex and watched his eyes light up. He examined the envelope, and seeing no return address, he remarked on it, and then slipped the letter out to read it. When he finished, he looked up and asked, "What do you think of this?"

Whether he was testing me to see if I'd noticed something he had or just wanted my opinion I couldn't tell, but I wanted to show him I'd paid attention to the details. Pointing at the bottom of the page, I said, "It's anonymous. No name and no return address either. I can't tell if it's a female's or male's handwriting, though."

Slowly, a smile crept onto his mouth. "You act like that's something definitive."

"Men usually have thinner handwriting, if they write in cursive at all. Most men I know print most of what they write. Women have rounder, loopier handwriting. This, though, seems to be almost part male and part female with the thinner parts on Candy's name and the rounder parts on some of the words toward the end. Weird."

He didn't say anything for a few seconds and then nodded. "I didn't come across too many handwritten notes in my time on the force. Very few people handwrite much of anything these days."

Pointing toward the letter in his hand, I looked over the writing on the page. "I know. It's becoming a lost art. Everyone texts and emails anymore."

"So who do you think wrote this? And why?"

I thought for a moment before saying, "I'm not sure about the who, but I can tell you why. Candy Skerrit had a Mount Rushmore-sized grudge against Geneva. She vowed to get revenge on her for cheating her out of tips and always being rude to her."

Narrowing his eyes as if to consider what I'd just said, he asked, "Is this another one of those gossip tales everyone in town but me knows?"

I chuckled at the idea that I had become someone in Sunset Ridge who'd be in the know like that. Like I was someone in the inner circle now.

"No. I found that out when I went to Candy's hair salon today. She runs Candy's Cuts on the other side of town, so I figured after I got that letter that I'd stop over and see if I could find out anything from her while she did my hair."

He lifted his gaze to look at my hair and smiled again. "It looks very nice. Very different from what you usually look like, in fact."

I had no idea if I should take that as a compliment or not, and after a second or two of wondering, I pushed it out of my mind to continue telling him about my fact-finding visit to Candy's Cuts.

"From what I found out, Candy and Geneva had a hate-hate relationship. Even though she insulted Candy every time she had her cut her hair, Geneva kept coming back. She refused to tip her too."

Clearly skeptical, Alex smirked. "Doesn't really sound like enough to make someone want to kill a person, though."

"You have no idea how much hatred one woman can have for another."

"Okay. I won't argue with you on that. As far as I can tell, women hating one another seems to be instinctual in your sex."

I held my hands up in front of me. "Don't put that on me. There are many women like me who don't work like that. Candy and Geneva aren't two of them, though."

He took a drink of his scotch and thought for a moment. "I don't understand why Geneva would keep returning to Candy to get her hair done if she hated it every time."

"Well, Candy is the best in town, and I can see someone like Geneva thinking she deserved the best of everything. It could have been something else, though. For what it's worth, I'd never heard anything about a feud between them until today, but that doesn't mean much. I'm not exactly in the know in this town."

Chuckling, he took another sip of his drink. "You underestimate yourself, Poppy. You know a lot about what goes on in this town. You and your father. Are you sure you never heard anything about them before?"

I shook my head, sure I knew no more than I'd found out that afternoon. "No. All I've ever known is that Candy is known around town as very rude. She likes to think she's being truthful, but as with most people who claim that, she can be quite blunt. She's offended many a person here in Sunset Ridge."

Even more confused, he asked, "Then why do people continue to go back to her to get their hair done?"

"Because she's the best."

"It must be a woman thing. If the guy who cuts my hair gave me a hard time, I'd just find someone else to do it. I'm paying him. The least he can do if he decides to talk at all is be pleasant."

"If only the world was run by men instead of emotional and erratic women," I joked sarcastically.

Now it was his turn to surrender in the conversation.

"Point taken. So did you find out anything else while Candy was doing your hair this afternoon?"

I opened my bag and took out my little notebook I'd written everything down in when I returned home. "Candy vowed to get revenge on Geneva for calling her, and I'm quoting here, 'a ham-handed, second-rate barber' before she stormed out last Friday. That was just two days before the murder."

"Did her hair look that bad when you saw her Monday morning?" Alex asked in a moment of odd curiosity about something unimportant.

Thinking back to when I saw her lying dead on her dining room floor, I shrugged. "Not really. It looked the same as it always did, except it was on a dead woman."

He gave me a tiny smile as a reward for my joke that was probably in poor taste and continued to explore what I'd found out that afternoon. "Did Candy say anything else to you about Geneva? Maybe that she wanted to kill her?"

"No such luck, but her assistant Kira told me something interesting. She said it looked like Candy wanted to wring her neck that last time she was there. She chased after her out onto the sidewalk after she insulted her."

The waiter brought our dinner and set our plates down in front of us as Alex remarked, "Interesting choice of words. Do you think Candy would be capable of killing her over that?"

I looked up to see the young man who'd delivered our meal wide-eyed at Alex's comment and smiled. "Thank you. It looks lovely."

He left quickly, likely frightened by our conversation, and I leaned forward toward Alex to warn him. "I think you scared our waiter with your talk of killing in front of him. Remember where you are. There are open ears everywhere, but especially here."

As he cut into his steak, he winked. "I'm counting on it. Let's eat and then over dessert I can tell you what I found out this afternoon."

"Okay. I'm not sure what you're up to, but I have to know. Do you think Candy is our third suspect? Can we add her to Shelley Steadman and Jefferson Girard?"

Alex closed his eyes as he took a bite of steak and nodded. "This is great steak."

I hated when he played games with me like that. Frustrated, I asked him again if Candy was our third suspect, and when he opened his eyes I saw I hadn't been wrong about her.

"I think she can be considered a suspect. Good job checking her out. Two questions, though, and then we'll get to this delicious meal. Did she have opportunity to commit the crime and did she have the means?"

I didn't have to think about the means part. I'd taken a look at Candy's arms as she styled my hair and saw she possessed some serious upper arm strength. At the very least she could strangle someone like Geneva, who was smaller than she was. As for the opportunity, that I didn't know, unfortunately.

"I don't know where she was Sunday night, but I think she could strangle a woman like Geneva, both because she hated her and she was bigger than our victim."

Savoring another bite of his New York Strip, he finished chewing and said, "Then we have another suspect. Now we'll just have to find out if we can put her at Geneva's during the time of the crime."

I cut into my bourbon pork chop and took a bite of the incredible food, but no matter how wonderful dinner was, it couldn't beat how great I felt about my work that afternoon. I might not have been a detective for real yet, but I was learning.

AFTER THE WAITER cleared our dishes and offered the dessert menu, Alex and I sat at our table in the center of Diamanti's satisfied after a wonderful dinner. The main dining room had filled up while we ate, so now we were surrounded by tables full of people whose own talking made any discussion of our case far more difficult now.

"Are you going to get dessert?" he asked. "I hear the cheesecake is to die for."

I couldn't help but laugh at the way he said that. "To die for? Is that some kind of inside joke because of our case?"

Realizing his unintended pun, he shook his head and smiled. "No, but it fits, doesn't it? I heard someone in line at the supermarket say that today, so I was mimicking her."

"Do you always listen to everything that's said around you?"

"Yes. I find out a lot of interesting tidbits of information that way. Like for example, I found out today that our police chief has recently been seen here on Wednesday and Thursday nights, and since I see our former mayor just walked in, I wonder if we'll see anything with them tonight."

Suddenly, it all made sense. That's why we were there.

"So that's why you invited me to dinner tonight?" I

asked, hating the surprise so evident in my voice. I should have been able to figure out this whole thing had something to do with our case.

"Yes," he said as he scanned the restaurant before returning his gaze to me. "I thought it might be a good place to see any fireworks between Dominick and the mayor."

I looked around for any sign of the chief but didn't see him. "Why would you think there would be any fireworks between them tonight?"

"Because Dominick was clearly a bit overzealous this morning when he found out Jefferson Girard might have something to do with this case. I'm betting if he's had a few drinks, he might say something to the mayor that could help us figure out if Jefferson Girard had a part in our murder."

I had no idea if the police chief was as big a drinker as Girard, but if they were both drunk we might get to see some spectacle right there. "Ah, so you're hoping this is more like dinner and a show."

Nodding, he gave me a grin. "Exactly. Clearly there's some problem between the two men, and my gut says it's more than just the former mayor cheating on his taxes. If that's all it was, Dominick wouldn't have been so eager to have one of the most important people in town dragged in for questioning at the first chance. No, there's something between them that isn't right, and I'm hoping from what I heard at the supermarket today about the possibility that both of them would be here at the same time tonight that we might get a clue or two what that something is."

"So you're thinking Dominick might unknowingly have information that would point to Jefferson Girard as

Geneva's killer?"

Alex merely arched an eyebrow as the former mayor and his wife walked past us to their table near the bar. I didn't want to turn around and be obvious, so I waited for him to tell me what he was watching so intently. He didn't, making me crazy with curiosity, and finally I repositioned my chair as casually as I could to see what was going on.

The mayor and his wife sat with their drinks as the waiter took their orders, and as soon as he walked away from the table, Dominick came storming toward them with a look of determination.

Turning to face Alex, whose gaze was focused on the scene unfolding in front of us, I asked, "What's going on?"

He raised his finger to this lips to tell me to be quiet and mouthed, "Watch," so I turned back around and listened as the police chief spoke to former Mayor Girard.

"I knew you were a cheat, but I didn't think you had murder in your bag of tricks, Jefferson. Once my brother and I have the proof, you're going down."

And then he stomped off out of the restaurant before the former mayor could even begin to respond to his accusation. Stunned at Dominick's outburst, I saw Alex's expression looked anything but surprised.

"Did you see that? I've never seen Dominick act like that. He seems like a man possessed. He and Derek must know something about Girard and the case, don't you think?"

He just smiled. "Very interesting. The more time I spend in this town, the more intrigued I am."

"I have a feeling our former mayor isn't going to just

get out of this with a slap on the wrist. Dominick looks like he's out for blood."

Alex raised his eyebrows and took a sip of his scotch. "Interesting, but I'm not as sure of Jefferson Girard's guilt as our police chief is. Then again, who am I compared to the chief of police of Sunset Ridge?"

Chapter Fourteen

I TOSSED AND turned all night as my brain tried to wrap itself around the idea that the former mayor of Sunset Ridge, Jefferson Girard, may have murdered Geneva Woodward. Yes, he was one of our suspects, but to be honest, I'd never considered him the most likely of the three. I didn't know why, but I found it hard to accept that he and not one of the two women had strangled poor Geneva right there in her finely appointed dining room. I had thought the killer had been a male at first, but now I wasn't sure.

As I lay there in bed watching the first rays of sunlight break the horizon, I wondered about something else. Was he the mystery man Shelley had seen sneaking into the back door of Geneva's house for a midnight rendezvous?

I instinctively twisted my face into a grimace at that rather disturbing thought. Jefferson Girard had never struck me as a sexy, clandestine meeting type of man. I'd always considered him more of a pudgy, smarmy political type most people tolerated more than liked. The idea of someone like Geneva being romantically involved with him stretched the imagination to a place I found difficult to believe, but then again, I hadn't seen her in any sexual way before this case either.

Stranger things had happened, though, so just because I couldn't imagine the two of them together didn't mean it was impossible. They said politics made strange bedfellows. Maybe it was a case of exactly that. Geneva did have the Woodward family money, and like most politicians, Jefferson Girard had always seemed like he was running for office, so perhaps he'd needed her to bankroll his campaigns and she'd needed him to…

Again, my brain returned to the image of them together, and I cringed. I simply couldn't imagine Geneva with her flowing blond hair and svelte body bumping up against Sunset Ridge's former mayor and his doughy self.

In addition to my inability to imagine them ever getting together, there was the fact that Girard had just expressed a real dislike for Geneva two nights before when Alex and I talked to him at my father's bar. What was that he said? She was the type to always complain?

I needed to speak to the woman who'd been his assistant during the entire time he was in office. I'd met her only once, but it had been in passing and I didn't even think I remembered her name. I'd have to find out when I went into work.

Reaching over to the nightstand, I grabbed my phone and saw a message from Oliver, my boss at The Bottom Line, reminding me that my work on the Pennsylvania politician story was due the day before. Damn! I hadn't so much forgotten it as gotten preoccupied with working on the case with Alex.

Who was I kidding? I'd forgotten all about my deadline. Quickly, I keyed in a message to him promising my work by end of today and pressed SEND.

My work at The Bottom Line may not have been that important, but it was my job and I always tried to do my best. At least I always had until this murder case and I partnered up with Alex. I needed to remember how important my word was and find a way to fit my research for The Bottom Line into my schedule.

I typed in a message to Alex about going to speak to Girard's assistant and asking him to join me and sent it off. Maybe he'd come up with some ideas overnight too that he'd share with me when we met for our morning coffee at The Grounds.

Our morning coffee. In such a short time, I'd begun to think of my trip to the coffee shop every morning not as merely a stop on my way to work but as a chance to speak to him about the case. I didn't know how it happened, but after only a few days he'd become someone I looked forward to seeing every day.

As I rolled out of bed to head to the shower, I couldn't help think it was odd how quickly we'd become the type of friends who thought of each other like that. Well, assuming he thought of me like that. I honestly didn't know what he thought of me. Had dinner the night before at Diamanti's been a date? I didn't think so when all was said and done, but there had been moments during the night that he acted more like a man taking me out than a partner having me join him on a case.

It didn't really matter what it had been because we'd gotten some important information about one of our suspects, and I intended on following up on that as soon as I'd had my morning coffee.

THE MORNING WORKING stiff crowd had cleared out of The Grounds by the time I'd gotten there just before nine o'clock. Nearly all the empty tables were littered with dirty plates and empty coffee cups, so I headed toward the one in the back of the shop where Alex and I had sat the day before and threw my bag on one of the chairs to save it just in case anyone other than he decided they wanted to join me. Desperate to get some caffeine into my system, I bought my coffee and returned to the table.

Taking my seat, I waited for Alex as I realized I didn't know how he took his coffee so I could have it waiting for him when he arrived. Mentally kicking myself for not picking up on that detail, I looked over at Jennie wiping down the bagel toaster and asked, "Jennie, how does Alex take his coffee each morning?"

Scrunching up her face, she thought for a long moment and said, "Hmmm. You know, I'm not sure. He's gotten a few different coffee blends recently, but I think I remember he always gets them with extra cream."

"Okay. Thanks."

"Don't you know? You've been in here a couple times with him and he knows how you take yours already," she said, not knowing how lame I felt that I hadn't noticed.

"I'll make sure to pay attention to exactly what he gets when he comes in today," she said with a smile before she returned to cleaning after the morning rush.

Me too, I thought as I sipped on my dark roast.

By ten, not only had he not arrived but he hadn't answered my text either. Unsure what could be holding him up, I texted again.

Hey, I'm at The Grounds. I had an idea about the mayor I wanted to share with you. See you in a few?

As I sat waiting for his text back, I wondered where he could be. When he'd walked me to my door after dinner, he hadn't seemed odd or unhappy. He had been quiet on the drive from Diamanti's, but that wasn't strange for Alex. Quiet seemed to be his natural state.

I heard someone come in and looked up from staring at my phone, but it wasn't him. A few more people came in and gave Jennie a mini-rush for mid-morning, but none of them were Alex either. By ten-thirty, I couldn't wait any longer if I wanted to finish up all the work I had to do for the day. I checked my phone one last time to see if I'd mistakenly turned off notifications. I hadn't and he'd never answered either of my two texts, so I reluctantly left the shop, missing my chance to talk about our case with him.

After a short but pointed discussion with my editor about how important the ladies of the Founders' Day committee were to the paper, I returned to my office at *The Eagle* and began my search for Jefferson Girard's former assistant's name. It didn't take long, and after skimming a few articles in the paper's database, I had my answer.

Jeannette McMurphy worked for then Mayor Jefferson Girard for ten of his twelve years in office. She left her job just before accusations of his tax cheating surfaced and retired to live a life of part-time volunteer work at the Sunset Ridge Memorial Library.

So that's where I would look for her first.

But before I could leave to walk the three blocks down Main Street to the town's library, Bethany popped in with an expectant look on her face. I knew what she was curious about. Too bad I didn't have anything to really tell her.

She sat down in the chair next to my desk and immediately asked, "So what happened? Did you wear the little black dress like I said? What did he wear? Tell me everything!"

"There's nothing to tell. I'm sorry to disappoint you, but I have no details."

Bethany's eyes grew wide. "Did he stand you up? God, men are pigs! I swear there isn't a good one left in the world. I'm so sorry, Poppy."

I held my hand up to stop her attack on Alex. "No, no. He didn't stand me up. We went out for dinner, just as planned. He had the steak and I had the bourbon pork chop. It was nice but nothing happened."

Crestfallen, she slumped in the chair. "Oh. Nothing happened?"

"Not a thing," I answered half-truthfully, sure she had no interest in the scene we'd witnessed between Dominick and the mayor or our discussion of Candy Skerrit's being a suspect.

Her blue eyes looked at me full of concern. "I don't understand. Why would he ask you out to dinner at Diamanti's and then do nothing? Maybe he's shy."

Closing my laptop, I pushed my chair away from my desk and stood up to leave. "We're friends, Bethany. That's all. It's no big deal."

She stood and looked at me. "So you're saying if I made the moves on him and we started dating that you'd be okay with that?"

"I guess," I said, unsure of where she was going with this. "But you don't even know him."

She smiled. "I saw him yesterday afternoon. He's delicious and I was going to keep my distance because I knew you were going out with him last night, but if he's on the market…"

I cut her off before she went any further. "I have no say in what Alex does, so go for it."

As I walked away from her, I couldn't put my finger on it, but I suddenly felt unhappy, which was stupid since Bethany was one of my closest friends and a great person. Why shouldn't she date Alex, who was a great guy?

THE SUNSET RIDGE Memorial Library was located in the oldest building in town, the former Northern Maryland Abolitionist Society building. Classically designed with a red brick face, it stood out against the rest of Main Street, which had changed over the years to be more modern.

I walked in and inhaled deeply, as I always did when I entered a library. For me, the smell of books brought back a feeling of comfort from my childhood that always reminded me of my mother. Every Saturday morning, we'd make our weekly pilgrimage to get a new book for me to cherish for the upcoming seven days. Then every night before I went to bed, my mother would sit on the edge of my twin bed and read to me. When I got old enough to read well enough on my own, she still sat there with me every night and listened to me tell that week's story. It was one of my favorite childhood memories.

The elderly librarian with the white hair and rosy cheeks behind the circulation desk gave me a knowing smile and a tiny wave. A fixture since I was a little girl, Mrs. Olsen hadn't seen me in years, but she still recognized me, probably because of how much I resembled my mother with my long light brown hair and blue eyes.

"Poppy McGuire! How are you?" she asked as I walked toward her desk in the center of the main room.

"I'm good, Mrs. Olsen. This place always smelled so great, and it still does."

She smiled in that gentle old lady way she always had and sighed. "You were one of my favorite little bookworms. I remember you coming in every Saturday with your mother. You were always so excited to get a new book, and she was one of our staunchest supporters."

"She was. She loved this library."

Mrs. Olsen's mouth turned down into a frown between her chubby cheeks. "When so many people in town didn't want to give to the library fund because they didn't think we served a purpose since computers were everywhere, she was right there at the fundraisers convincing people to give whatever they could because no matter what, she believed libraries were one of the most important places in a town. I still remember her saying that to Mrs. Scanlon right before she got out that checkbook of hers to make a donation."

That was my mother. Always fighting for a cause. I loved that about her, and it was nice to hear people outside my family had appreciated that about her too.

For a moment, Mrs. Olsen and I stood there each remembering her in our own way. Finally, I broke the silence before I got too lost in my memories of all those Saturdays.

"I'm looking for Jeannette McMurphy, Mrs. Olsen. I was told she still volunteers here. Is she in today?"

"She is," she said as she walked around her desk to point toward the side room where the stacks were located. "You should be able to find her in the cookbooks."

Thanking her, I headed toward where she'd pointed to and just a few steps into the stacks found who I was looking for. A tiny woman, Jeannette McMurphy reminded me of one of those China dolls that used to be popular. She had a dainty look to her, and when she turned to look at me, I couldn't help but be struck by how smooth her face was for a woman who was said to be in her early sixties.

"Can I help you?" she asked in a little voice that matched her frame perfectly.

"I'm Poppy McGuire, Mrs. McMurphy. Do you have a minute to talk to me? I wanted to ask you a few questions about your time as the mayor's assistant."

She looked up at me with faded brown eyes and nodded. "You're from the newspaper, aren't you? Are you doing some kind of write-up on him?"

I'd planned on easing into my questions, but looking around, I didn't see a chair I could sit in and there didn't seem to be a better time than the present, so I dove in and said, "Not exactly. I'm hoping you can tell me if he knew Geneva Woodward."

A look of recognition flashed in her eyes and she took a deep breath in. "Knew her? She was the bane of his existence. Well, one of them. That woman, God rest her soul, was difficult."

"What was the problem between the two of them?"

"Oh, what wasn't the problem? One time she

demanded to see him about her neighbor's dogs. They were keeping her up nights with their barking. Another time she insisted that he do something about the parking situation in the alley way behind her house."

I thought back to when Alex and I went to check out that alley. Far too narrow to fit even two cars at the same time, it was more of a walking path than anywhere really meant for driving or parking.

"What was the problem?"

Mrs. McMurphy sighed. "There was a car that parked there every Sunday for a few hours behind one of her neighbors' houses, and she wanted that stopped. She didn't think it was safe because the alley way was grass and not wide enough for cars, if I remember correctly."

"These don't sound like more than nuisances, though. Not really bane of someone's existence kind of stuff."

"It wasn't so much the complaints as the way she made them. She'd storm into the office, walking right past me, and interrupt the mayor. It didn't matter who he was in there with. She'd just start complaining loudly, and one time she even yelled at him. Every week, you could expect her to come in and be unhappy with something at least once."

"Interesting. It's strange that she didn't go to the police with some of her complaints. The parking issue probably would have been something they could handle."

Mrs. McMurphy nodded. "It was like that with a lot of her complaints, and every time she came in to see the mayor she always sounded like my mother-in-law did when she yelled at my father-in-law. I actually asked him one time if he'd been married to her in a previous life.

You know, as a joke because her complaining always sounded so personal. But he wasn't the type of man to ever marry a woman like that, not in this life or any other."

"Do you remember anything else about when they'd be together in his office all those times she came in to complain? Is there any chance things ever got nicer between them?"

"No. If anything, they got worse. By the time I left, she was coming in a few times a week and she was full of venom every single time."

"One more thing, Mrs. McMurphy. Who replaced you after you left the mayor's office?"

"Nobody. The mayor didn't think he could find anyone who could do my job like I could, so he had his wife take over when I left."

Geneva's constant complaining may have gotten to the mayor, but if that was the case, why did he wait all these months to kill her, I wondered. Thanking Mrs. McMurphy, I headed back to my office to see if I could find out if there was any connection between Geneva and Jefferson Girard in that time after his assistant left since I certainly couldn't ask the woman who'd replaced her.

I was thankful Bethany had left on one of her client visits by the time I returned so I wouldn't have to discuss Alex being single and available any further. I didn't know why, but the whole time I was walking back to *The Eagle*'s offices my stomach felt like it was in a tight knot.

Using the newspaper's database once more, I searched for articles on the mayor and hoped I might be able to find something. It was unlikely the town newspaper would have printed anything derogatory about Jefferson Girard. To say *The Sunset Ridge Eagle* was partisan would be an understatement, to say the least.

But if I could find some lead in a newspaper from elsewhere in the county that had been far less complimentary during his tax cheating scandal, I might be able to get a sense of what happened in those few months after Jeannette McMurphy left the mayor's office.

I searched for over an hour and found nothing more than I already knew about Jefferson Girard. One article stood out, though. He had ruffled some feathers in the neighboring areas when he refused to help out the town next to us after their firehouse burned down in a horribly ironic fire, which thankfully had hurt no one but completely destroyed their only firetruck.

If Girard had been the one murdered, there was yet another reason for a murderer to off him, but none of that had anything to do with Geneva. Article after article said much of the same. Passable mayor who did questionable things.

Rubbing my bleary eyes after staring at my laptop screen for so long, I wished for some kind of divine intervention to help me find something that would give me a lead to go on. Scrolling down the page of results, I got to the bottom and then clicked to the next page. By the time I was halfway done, I wondered if I'd ever find anything new on him.

But then toward the bottom of page two there it was. A picture of the mayor from at least twenty years ago. I excitedly clicked on the link and saw Jefferson Girard as a man of about thirty, but under the photo in the article was the name Jonas Gregory.

Was this a different man and the search results had

gotten confused because he looked so like Jefferson Girard during his tenure as mayor? The pudgy face looked very similar, but the man in the photo had more hair.

I read the article, my eyes racing over the words as I tried to ascertain if it was the very same man. A woman in a small Vermont town disappeared after being involved in a love triangle. This Jonas Gregory was the prime suspect since he'd been the other man who she cheated on her husband with. He was eventually cleared, but the scandal drove him out of town.

Had the former mayor been this Jonas Gregory man? My brain raced through all I knew about Jefferson Girard. For as long as I remembered, he'd lived in Sunset Ridge. Even back when I was a child, he was a resident in town.

Quickly I called my father to ask him what he knew about the former mayor. As soon as he answered, I blurted out, "Dad, has Jefferson Girard always lived in Sunset Ridge?"

"Poppy, what's wrong? You sound different."

"I just need to know if the former mayor has always lived here. Do you know?"

"Let me think. Well, he served in office for twelve years, so before being elected he had to be a citizen for at least a year to be eligible, I think. But always? I don't think so. He's around my age, and I don't remember him from high school. Why are you asking?"

My heart leaped at the idea that I'd found something. "Just checking things out. I'll talk to you later, okay?"

I hurried off the phone to get back to searching for even more information. Two pages of results later, I found something I wouldn't have expected in a million years. There in an article from that same small town newspaper in Vermont was a picture of none other than Geneva! I read like a madwoman to find out what her picture would be doing in an article titled Missing Woman From Notable Family.

Astonished, I saw that the Woodward family lived in that small Vermont town and Geneva's mother had only left there after her daughter went missing. The article was dated twenty-five years ago, but there could be no doubt. The woman who had disappeared was Geneva Woodward.

Chapter Fifteen

I RACED HOME to get my car so I could drive out to Alex's and tell him what I'd found. Since he hadn't answered any of my texts all day, I figured I wouldn't bother trying to get him that way again. This kind of news demanded an in-person telling anyway. I couldn't wait to see his face when I told him that former mayor Jefferson Girard and Geneva Woodward had a history!

Pulling up to his house, I found it looking much like it did the last time I was there. Even though it was still daylight out and his car was parked in the driveway, the place looked abandoned like no one was around. With each step toward the door, I grew more excited, though. Alex would see I had done my homework and found the clues to show that our murderer was Girard.

I'd all but solved this case for us, and I couldn't wait to hear what he had to say when I told him.

I knocked and waited, bouncing on my toes with excitement, but nobody answered. Had he gone out on foot? I knocked again, harder this time, and after a few seconds heard footsteps coming toward the door.

It opened just enough to let me see him standing there looking much like he always did, but in his eyes there was something odd in the way he stared out at me.

I couldn't put my finger on it, but he looked strange.

"Hey, I've been texting you all day. I have news. Can I come in?"

He hesitated for a few moments, but then he nodded and opened the door. Walking past him, I entered his living room and waited for him to offer me a drink and a seat. But he did neither. He simply closed the door and turned to face me.

"What's going on, Poppy?" he asked in a somber voice.

"I found something out about our case that I wanted to share with you. I figured we could go to Derek with it after and then maybe a celebratory bite to eat. You know, because it's my first case and I blew it wide open."

"Yeah?"

His almost complete lack of interest in what I had to tell him baffled me. Alex had never been overly enthusiastic in all the time I'd spent with him, but I'd at least expected him to want to hear what I had to say, especially since I'd just alluded to solving the case.

"Alex, what's wrong? Did something happen?"

I wasn't sure what could have happened to make him so disinterested in solving Geneva Woodward's murder since not twenty-four hours earlier he'd intentionally gone to Diamanti's just for the case. Was that it? Had I done something at dinner that had upset him?

"I just...I'm just not really up to dealing with the case today," he said in that same somber voice that matched the unhappiness written all over his face.

Suddenly I felt unwelcome in his home once again. Uncomfortable and feeling foolish that I'd let myself believe we'd become close friends, I stammered out,

"I'm…I mean I'm…I didn't mean to intrude. I just thought you might want to know what I found."

We stood there awkwardly staring at one another for so long I felt like running out and speeding away, but then he quietly offered me a seat and sat down in a chair across from me. We hadn't been like this around one another since that first night he found me in his backyard, and I couldn't understand what had happened to change things.

Then an idea popped into my head. Had last night been a date and I hadn't acted interested, so now he didn't feel right about working with me on the case?

I hated thinking like that. If I hurt or offended him, I wasn't sure if I should bring it up or just leave it alone.

Or maybe I was completely off the mark and something else was the problem, something that had nothing to do with me or our time at Diamanti's last night.

"What did you want to tell me, Poppy?"

As clear as day, I heard his voice catch when he said my name. Had I done something? I didn't know, and the stern look in his eyes told me he probably wouldn't tell me if I had anyway.

"I found out that Jefferson Girard and Geneva had a history. Jeannette McMurphy, the woman who worked for him, told me Geneva practically badgered him at least once a week when he was the mayor." Waving the paper with the article about the missing woman and the love triangle, I said, "And then there's this about her in Vermont."

Alex held his hand up to stop me. "Wait. What are you talking about? What history?"

"Geneva constantly harangued Girard while he was

in office. Even his secretary thought it seemed personal."

"I imagine small town mayors get that kind of thing all the time, Poppy," he said, practically dismissing what I'd said. "What are you talking about something with Geneva in Vermont?"

"Up in Vermont. They both lived there in the same town. They were involved."

"Involved? Like what?" he asked, perking up for the first time since he opened the door and saw me standing there.

"Like romantically! She was married and having an affair, and the person she was having an affair with was none other than the former mayor himself. Can you believe it?"

His eyes opened wide, and it looked like the Alex I'd been spending all that time with had returned. Holding out his hand, he said, "Interesting. Let me see."

I handed him the printouts of the articles I'd found and knew he'd see that this case had totally been turned on its head. He looked down at the paper and read the details of Jefferson Girard before he came to Sunset Ridge. His response wasn't exactly as thrilled as I had hoped for, but this was Alex, after all. He wasn't the type of man who ever jumped up and screamed for joy.

Because he seemed to not be entirely convinced, I showed him the pictures of the much younger versions of the mayor and Geneva, laying them out on the coffee table in front of him. "You can see they're both the same people. He went under a different name, but her name was the same back there."

Alex studied the pictures, first leaning forward to look at them and then lifting each one to eye level to examine it even closer. What was he looking for?

When he didn't say anything, I said, "Are you thinking they were photoshopped? Why would anyone do that?"

He remained silent for a few more moments and then lowered the paper from in front of his face to show me his look of skepticism I'd seen before. Was he serious? How could he be skeptical now that I'd shown him all this new information?

"I don't know. Why would anyone do anything?"

I leaned away from him, unsure of what he was referring to. Who asked questions like that? "I have no idea how to answer that, Alex. All I know is that both Girard and Geneva lived in the same town up in Vermont and were involved in a love triangle. They knew each other, and the way I'm seeing it, pretty intimately."

He pointed at the article on the table about the missing woman. "Did you read all the way to the end of that?"

I thought I had, but what did it matter? I knew what journalists stuck at the end of a piece. Nothing useful since readers often didn't make it that far. So what was he talking about?

"Yes. Why?"

Handing it to me, he said, "Read it again. I think you missed something."

I didn't like what I saw as smugness on his face, and taking the piece of paper from his hold, I quickly moved my gaze to the bottom of the page. What exactly did he think I'd missed?

Update: We are saddened to report that the victim, Geneva Woodward, was found dead on June 22.

Letting the paper drop into my lap, I looked up at

him and saw that same smugness that now made me want to dig my heels in even more. I didn't care what that newspaper said. I knew what I knew.

"So you're okay with believing that someone would alter a picture but not with the idea that the wrong information could be printed in a newspaper article?"

My question didn't faze him in the least. He continued to stare at me like I was the biggest fool he'd ever met. But I had no intentions of just crumbling under his withering glare I knew was meant to chastise me for being sloppy, or whatever he thought I was.

"Poppy, it says the missing woman was found dead. How can that be our victim, who up to just a few days ago was alive and well and living in Sunset Ridge?"

Frustrated, I felt all the enthusiasm for sharing my findings with Alex drain out of my body. Yes, he was right. The article did say that the missing woman had been found dead. Then an idea came to me.

"Fine. She was found dead. If that's the truth, then why wasn't the prime suspect in her disappearance then made the prime suspect in her murder? I found nothing in the database that followed up on this. Don't you think I would have?"

Alex didn't have an answer to that, but it didn't change the fact that he thought I was wrong. With a shrug, he said, "I'm not sure. Maybe you didn't search the right way for that information to come up on the database?"

Was he serious? Did he actually say I didn't know how to search for information, the one key part of my job for The Bottom Line?

Incensed at his casual insult, I pointed my finger at him and let him have it. "I'm sure you didn't just say that I don't know how to do my job. I've been researching for years, and I think I know how to use a damn database. You just don't want to admit I'm right on this because you don't think Jefferson Girard is the right suspect. Well, in this case, you're wrong, Mr. Fantastic Detective."

My outburst stunned him, but he quickly regrouped. Folding his arms across his chest, he said in an all-too-calm voice, "What about the fact that we have a letter pointing to Candy Skerrit as a suspect and that her assistant said she wanted to wring Geneva's neck? We haven't even found out who wrote that letter yet."

Was he actually saying some note anyone could have written to implicate one of the rudest women in town was worth as much of our attention as the evidence I had right in my hands?

"I want to tell you a story about when I was on the force that I think you need to hear."

Something told me I didn't need to hear whatever it was he wanted to tell me, but I sat back in my seat and figured I'd give him a chance to enlighten me.

"Poppy, a lot of times it seems like a detective is onto the clue that will break a tough case, but the problem is that often it's just a lead to nowhere. That's what I think this is. When I was on the force, I was involved in a case that kept giving the lead detective dead ends. His wife was murdered, so he was rightly hell bent on finding the killer and bringing him to justice. But all the leads turned out to be nothing."

I wanted to stop him before he went any further, but before I could say anything, he took a breath and continued.

"Every time one of those leads turned up, he was

sure it would be the one that would blow the case wide open. He'd go running around after it on what would end up as wild goose chases over and over, even though his fellow detectives kept telling him to slow down and take a step back. He couldn't, though. He was too close to the case, so he couldn't see the truth of things. There were better officers who could have taken the case, but he wouldn't let them. He couldn't distance himself."

"And you think I'm too close to this case?" I asked sharply, not even trying to temper my anger at him.

"I think so. If you weren't, you'd see that the woman you think was Geneva couldn't be her. I'm not even sure the younger man in the picture you showed me was the former mayor."

I jumped to my feet as furious indignation coursed through my body. Unable to control my emotions, I barked, "You know what I think? I think that story of yours is more appropriate to your situation with your wife's death and has nothing to do with me. If you don't want to believe in me on this, then fine. I don't need your help with this case or anything else!"

His expression morphed from stunned at my explosion of anger to hurt at my mention of his wife. I didn't care, though. Whatever he was dealing with, he was putting his issues onto our murder case and muddling it because he couldn't separate his past from the present. That wasn't my fault, and I wouldn't stand there to be lectured to when it was him who needed to take his own advice.

Storming away, I flung his front door open and stomped down the front stairs, not even caring that I'd left all the information on his coffee table. I could get more copies of all of it, so it didn't matter.

By the time I sat down behind the wheel, the adrenaline rush that had pumped through my veins had subsided, and I sat there deflated and wishing none of it had happened. I watched as his front door slowly closed and felt like I'd lost a friend, but even more, I felt like I'd hurt someone intentionally who hadn't deserved it.

ALL AFTERNOON, I worked to forget how awful I felt about what I said to Alex while I spied on Jefferson Girard's comings and goings. I watched him putter around his backyard planting flowers, walk to the grocery store for cold cuts and bread, and then back to his house for more landscaping. I honestly wondered if I may have been wrong about him as I saw him spend his time like a stereotypical retiree.

I had to push that out of my mind, though. Even murderers could love to plant flowers and eat sandwiches.

By dinnertime, I hadn't seen him do anything I could use to prove my assertion that he was Geneva's murderer, so I decided to take another tactic. I took a slow walk to her neighborhood three blocks away and looked for any of the people who lived around her to talk to. Four houses away from Geneva's house I found a woman named Sarah and asked her if she'd seen anyone she recognized around Geneva's the night of the murder, but she didn't remember seeing anyone and fell asleep before eleven that night.

Across the street from the murder scene, the owner of a house that faced Geneva's, Jacob Minton, told me he was up for much of the night and saw lights on throughout the house, but he didn't think he'd seen anyone Sunday night either.

I left him watering his lawn and tried to keep faith in my gut feeling about Jefferson Girard being the one who killed Geneva, even though I couldn't find anyone to say they'd seen anyone lurking around the neighborhood that night. That I had no real idea what his motive was had occurred to me too.

Actually, motive was the least of my concerns. The combination of their past in Vermont and their history while he was in office surely would equal some reason why he'd want to kill her. Maybe she was planning to tell the truth about their relationship up north and he didn't want his wife to find out. Or maybe she wanted him back after all those years they'd lived so close to one another in town and he had to kill her to stop her from ruining his life that way.

Whatever it was, I believed Jefferson Girard was the killer.

Around six o'clock, I came upon Gertrude Jenkins sitting on her porch enjoying the unseasonably warm evening weather. An elderly woman with teased blond hair and a thin face, she had been one of the secretaries at Sunset Ridge High School when I was a student there. I hoped she'd remember me and be willing to talk about what she may have seen that fateful night since she lived directly behind Geneva.

Waving to her from the street, I yelled, "Hi, Mrs. Jenkins! How are you tonight?"

She strained to look at me, taking a few moments to recognize who I was, and finally answered, "Oh, is that you, Poppy? My eyesight isn't what it used to be. Come on up on the porch."

I joined her on the porch swing and after we talked a

little about the old days at Sunset Ridge High, I asked her if she'd seen anything out of the ordinary the night of Geneva's murder.

Placing her hand on mine, she gave me a gentle smile. "I'm the wrong person to ask, but my granddaughter Alicia might know something. I'm in bed early by seven each night, although I love to watch my shows. She keeps later hours than I do. By the time that woman was murdered, I was sound asleep."

"Is Alicia here? I'd like to ask her some questions."

"She'll be home in a few hours, but let me call her to see when she can talk to you."

Gertrude Jenkins took out her cell phone from her apron and dialed her granddaughter. "Alicia, Poppy McGuire is here with me and wants to know if you saw anything out of the ordinary the night Geneva Woodward died."

I heard Alicia say she had, and Gertrude said to me, "She saw a man go to the back door of Geneva's. Oh yes, now I remember. She told me about him a few weeks ago, but as I said, I'm always asleep early."

"Can she meet with me after work?"

Alicia heard my question and answered her. "Yes, she says she can meet you at Madison Diner right after seven tonight. Oh, hang on. She wants to talk to you herself."

I took the phone from Gertrude and said, "Alicia, I can be there tonight. Thanks so much for being willing to talk to me."

"Poppy, don't tell my grandmother what I'm about to say, but that man who was coming to visit Geneva, I think I know who he is. I can't talk right now because there are people around, but I'll meet you right after seven at the diner, okay?"

"Okay. I'll see you then."

Handing the phone back to her grandmother, I thanked her and left to head back to my place for a little bit before it was time to meet Alicia. At a few minutes before seven, I walked down to the Madison Diner and found a booth in the back to wait nervously to hear what she had to say.

My mind raced thinking of who could be the mystery man Alicia had seen. Whoever it was, he could be the key to solving the case. If I was correct, he was none other than Jefferson Girard, the former mayor and murderer of Geneva Woodward, his former lover.

Two glasses of sweet tea later, I looked up at the clock on the far wall of the diner and saw it was already after eight. I hurried over to her grandmother's house just in case Alicia had to stop there after work and had gotten held up. I knocked on the front door for five minutes, but got no answer.

Something was wrong.

I walked around the outside of the house as I called the police station to ask Derek for his help, but Dominick answered. Knowing he'd probably read me the riot act, I lied and told him how she was supposed to meet me over an hour earlier and that I was concerned she might have gotten hurt. I hoped what I was feeling was misplaced disappointment over not hearing who Geneva's mystery man was, but my gut told me something bad had happened.

"Poppy, are you sure she knew you two were supposed to meet?"

"Yes, Dominick. Now please, can you come over to her grandmother's house behind Geneva's and check things out?"

"She might have gotten tied up with friends. This doesn't sound like a police emergency, Poppy. If I get a chance, I'll take a drive by the neighborhood a little later on."

Reluctantly, I explained what I believed about the mayor, hoping that his actions the night before at Diamanti's might mean he wouldn't force me off the case. "I think Alicia was going to tell me she saw Girard go into Geneva's the very night she was murdered. If she did and he found out somehow, she might be hurt or worse. Please hurry!"

"What are you doing involved in the Geneva Woodward case, Poppy? I've told you before how I feel—"

"Dominick! You can ream me out later, but for now, will you just do this for me and not give me chapter and verse about how I'm not supposed to stick my nose in your cases?"

Less than five minutes later, he arrived in his police cruiser and the two of us banged on her grandmother's front door, but no one answered. He tried the doorknob and found it unlocked. Poking his head in, he yelled Alicia's name but got no answer, so he drew his gun and slowly entered the house.

I followed, even though I knew he probably didn't want me to, and before we made it a few steps inside, we saw Alicia lying unconscious on the ground. He rushed over to her and checked for a pulse, but it was too late.

She was dead, silenced before she could tell me who she suspected of being Geneva's mystery man and very likely her murderer.

Chapter Sixteen

I LAY IN bed sobbing, unable to sleep all night to escape the thought that Alicia's death had been caused by my carelessness. All I could think of was how obvious I'd been watching the mayor all afternoon and then walking around Geneva's neighborhood asking questions to just anyone. What if one of those people had been the murderer and saw me sitting on the porch talking to Gertrude Jenkins? What if the murderer had overheard me make plans to meet with Alicia and decided then that she had to be silenced?

I'd been so sure of myself that I hadn't remembered at the heart of this case lay a murderer. How could I have been so stupid? Alex was right. I was too close to the case.

As the sunrise peeked through my bedroom window, all I felt was utter sadness. I didn't know how to go on, but I knew I needed to. Now more than ever, I had to find the one who murdered Geneva and most likely killed Alicia before she could tell me who he was.

Sunset Ridge's former mayor and Geneva's former lover Jefferson Girard looked guiltier than ever, and to make up for my part in Alicia's death, I had to prove he did it beyond a shadow of a doubt.

My alarm rang, shaking me from my misery for just a moment, and I quickly swiped my cell phone to stop the chimes that usually woke me so gently but now just sounded like funeral music. The message icon showed I had unread texts, and there right on top was one from my boss at The Bottom Line telling me my second missed deadline had passed.

When it rained, it poured.

Even worse, there were no new texts from Alex. Not that I should have expected any. After my outburst, I'd be lucky if he ever spoke to me again.

Waking up to a hat trick of misery like this was enough to make me want to stay in bed all day, but if I wanted to keep my job, I needed to finish my piece for my boss and get it to him before noon. The implied meaning in his message was if I didn't, I shouldn't bother to consider myself his employee any longer.

I dragged myself out of bed, praying this day would get better but not holding much hope for that. Even making myself a cup of my favorite morning pick-me-up didn't help. On top of feeling to blame for Alicia's death, I missed sitting with Alex at The Grounds and talking while I enjoyed my dark roast.

As I stood leaning against my kitchen counter still in my pajamas, a knock on my door startled me out of my misery, and I answered it to find my father standing on my welcome mat. The concerned look on his face told me he'd heard what happened.

Without saying a thing, he knew what I needed. Stepping toward me, he opened his arms wide and took me into them for a hug. Unable to stop the tears from coming once again, I sobbed against his shoulder as the weight of everything that had transpired the day before threatened to crush me.

"I know, honey. Let it out. Let it all out."

I let myself cry like I hadn't done since my mother died, and my father held me tightly in his arms as we stood there in my kitchen just like he had that awful day when the loveliest soul in my world left us.

Finally, after nearly ten minutes of doing exactly as he'd said and letting it all out, I looked up at him and wiped my eyes. "Thanks, Dad."

He smiled that gentle way he did when I skinned my knee as a little girl or got my heart broken by a teenage crush. "You want to talk about it?"

Taking a deep breath in, I felt much of my sadness ebb away and nodded. Maybe talking to someone about how awful I felt might help. "Yeah. You want some coffee?"

He stepped around me and pulled a chair out from the table. "You sit. I can get my own coffee. Is it that dark roast stuff you like to get at the coffee shop?"

I sat down and took a sip of my regular coffee from the grocery store. "No, just ordinary coffee. It's why I don't usually drink it here in the mornings anymore."

The thought of sitting across from Alex at a table at The Grounds flashed through my mind, and I sighed. Was he there right now, sitting alone at that back table we'd sat at nearly every time we went there? Or had someone joined him, one of the women in town eager to find out about this new guy nobody seemed to know much about?

My father sat down on the other side of the table and placed his coffee mug in front of him. "About that. Haven't you been going to The Grounds with Alex every morning? Why aren't you there talking about your case this morning?"

"We had a falling out," I mumbled as I looked away so he couldn't see how much what I'd done bothered me.

"Over the case? I'm sure it's nothing new for him. He was a detective for years, Poppy. I'm sure in all that time he had people disagree with his theory of a case now and again."

"It was something different. It started out about the case, but then it got…" I didn't finish my sentence because I couldn't explain why I'd exploded like I had. I'd never been really emotional, so I didn't know why I acted the way I did.

"Look at me, Elizabeth."

My father's voice was gentle but insisting, so I took a deep breath and slowly let it out as I turned my head to face him. "Yeah, Dad?"

"What's all this about? What's going on with you and Alex?"

"Nothing. It's not like that, Dad. We're just partners who are trying to find out who killed Geneva. Well, were partners."

My father's gentle smile returned. "For someone you've only known for a week, this seems to be a lot of sadness over a disagreement, don't you think?"

Hanging my head, I admitted what I felt. "I know it seems like we became close really fast, but that's just how it happened. I really admire him and I want to learn from him how he figures things out that other people don't see. I can't explain it, Dad, but I just like being around him."

"Are you sure it's nothing more? You two looked almost inseparable that night at the bar. People who only know each other for as short a time as you two have usually don't sit so close and lean on each other like you two were. If I didn't know better, I would have thought you two were romantically involved."

"No. We're not like that. He's still in love with the past, and I'm not looking for a boyfriend in him."

My father took hold of my hand and gently squeezed it. "Are you sure? I know what I saw."

"No, it's nothing like that, Dad. And now it's really nothing since we aren't speaking to one another, even though if there ever was a time I needed his help, it's now."

The look of concern my father had worn when he showed up at my door returned now. "Why? What's happened?"

Tears welled in my eyes again, and I struggled to keep myself from falling apart. "There was another murder last night."

"Another murder in Sunset Ridge? Who?"

"Alicia Jenkins. Do you remember Mrs. Jenkins from the high school? Her granddaughter. I think it was my fault she got killed, Dad."

Any chance of stopping the tears vanished as soon as the words left my mouth. I buried my face in my hands and let them come again.

"Poppy, you couldn't hurt a fly. How could you think it was your fault? Do we know who did it?"

I sniffled and tried to explain, but my crying made it difficult. "I think it was the same person who killed Geneva and they found out that Alicia was going to tell me who she thought the man was visiting Geneva late at night. I think he killed her to keep her from talking."

Handing me a napkin, my father knitted his brows in

that way he always did when his concern for me had turned to genuine worry. "You're going to get yourself hurt or worse, Poppy. Maybe it's time to let the police do their job and stop this."

He was probably right. It seemed likely that the killer knew I was onto him, so I was next if I kept sticking my nose into things.

"Maybe you're right. I don't know, Dad. It just feels like I shouldn't give up, especially now that someone got killed because of me."

"That didn't happen because of you, honey. She was murdered by someone who is evil. It's that simple. I'm just terrified that this same evil person is going to come after you."

I dried my eyes again and confessed my suspicions to the only person I could. "It's the mayor, Dad. Jefferson Girard."

My father had always been a rock compared to everyone else in my life. His strength and composure in the face of anything that came up, even my mother's death, had always been something I could rely on. But now as he sat staring at me with his mouth hanging open, he looked like he couldn't wrap his brain around what I'd said.

"I know. It sounds incredible, but it's him, Dad. Mayor Girard is the murderer. He killed Geneva because they had a relationship when they both lived in Vermont. I had always thought she lived in Sunset Ridge all her life, but I found out she lived up north and knew the mayor when he was named Jonas something."

"You know what? She didn't always live here. The Woodward family did, but she didn't. I hadn't thought of that. So you're saying he killed her and then he killed that girl because she knew he did it?"

My chest felt like someone was sitting on it, and I struggled to take a full breath in when I thought of that pudgy, middle-aged man sneaking up behind her and bashing her in the head as her poor grandmother slept just one floor up. She didn't deserve that.

"But if she knew who killed Geneva, why didn't she go to the police?"

"I don't know. I think she believed she knew who Geneva's mystery man was and wanted to tell me, but it's still not certain that he was the same person who killed her."

My father took the last gulp of his coffee and sighed. "I'm worried about you, Poppy. This is dangerous, and you're going to get hurt."

I stood and walked over to stand behind him to give him a reassuring hug. Nuzzling his unshaven neck like I did when I was a child, I tried to make him see why I had to do this. "I need to see this through to the end. You understand that, don't you?"

He turned his head to kiss me on the cheek and nodded. "I understand. You're just like your mother was. Once she got interested in something, she was like a dog with a bone."

Grabbing his coffee cup, I headed toward the sink to rinse it out. "Well, thank God for that or I might not be alive. You always have said she chased after you, even though she never liked it when you said that."

My father smiled broadly, as he always did when I mentioned that story. "She did. I was just some stupid kid who didn't know a great thing when he saw it. She was the one who had to show me what I was missing by not dating her."

I finished washing out his cup and placed it in the

dish rack. I liked thinking of my mother like that instead of how I usually thought of her as sick but fighting until the end. Whenever I had the chance to remember her before she fell ill, I always felt better afterward.

"Just promise me you're going to be safe, Poppy," he said as he came over to the sink to give me a goodbye hug.

"I promise, Dad. Derek and Dominick are always around anyway, and now that I'm not working with Alex, maybe I'll just stick by Derek's side until the case is over."

He leaned back away from me and cocked his eyebrow. "I'm sure Derek will love that. He's liked you a bit more than a friend should since grade school. As for Alex, I don't think you two are done quite yet. I saw something between you two at the bar the other night. Maybe I read it wrong and it's not romance. I think we both know I've been wrong on that subject before. But I saw what I saw. You two work well together. I'd hate to see that end over whatever happened."

I kissed my father goodbye and closed the door behind him as the sting of regret pinched at me over what I'd said to Alex. I'd been hurtful, and that wasn't me. So I had to fix it, or at least try.

Picking up my phone from the kitchen table, I texted him a message I hoped would make him see I really didn't mean what I'd said.

Hey, Alex. I'm sorry for what I said yesterday. I never intended to hurt you.

I waited twenty minutes for him to text back an answer. He never did.

By MID-AFTERNOON, I hadn't even showered or gotten out of my pajamas since I couldn't seem to shake the sadness about Alicia's death and what had happened with Alex. I knew I needed to because there was more work to do, though, so after a particularly rousing episode of one of those court shows where the judge is famous for some stupid catch phrase instead of meting out real justice, I pulled myself up off the couch and headed upstairs to get my day going.

Diamanti's opened at four, so I called at four o'clock on the nose to ask if the former mayor would be dining with them that night and to try to get a reservation. Thankfully, the woman who answered cared nothing for privacy, which wasn't surprising in Sunset Ridge, and freely gave up the information that he and his wife would be there by half past seven. So I asked if they could fit me in even though it was one of their busier nights, and I got an eight PM spot in the main dining room.

I fully intended to keep my eye on Girard, even though I'd told my father otherwise. I knew he'd worry himself needlessly if he thought I would be working alone, but teaming up with Derek just didn't sound like a good idea. He was nice enough and I was sure he had some detective skills inside that pretty head of his, but I didn't want to partner with someone else tonight.

At a few minutes after seven-thirty, I checked myself out for one last time in my bedroom mirror. Dressed in a pink sweater set, black pants, and flats, I didn't look as great as I had the other night, but I was aiming for comfort this time. If I needed to quickly follow Girard somewhere, I had to know I wouldn't get tripped up in high heels or a dress.

Not that I didn't look good, but tonight's look had a practicality to it that I hoped would come in handy.

The crowd milling about outside the front of Diamanti's made merely getting into the restaurant a hassle, so it was quarter after eight before I even got sat at my table. I scanned the dining room hoping I hadn't missed Jefferson Girard, but lo and behold there he was at a table near the bar with the First Lady, the two of them with drinks in their hands and big smiles on their faces as they raised their glasses in a toast.

My stomach roiled at the thought of him toasting to their happiness and long life while Geneva and Alicia lay dead by his hand. If it was the last thing I did, I'd see him pay for what he'd done.

Lost in thought at how wonderful it would be when he was finally behind bars, I didn't notice Derek sit down at my table until he cleared his throat. Surprised to see him across from me wearing his police uniform, I straightened in my seat and awaited the onslaught of reprimands he would give me for telling his brother I was helping with the case.

"How are you tonight, Poppy?" he asked in a voice that sounded a little too sweet for someone about to dress me down.

"I'm good, Derek. How are you?"

He seemed to think about my very basic question meant more as polite chit chat than anything else, and then he frowned. "I'm good, all things considered."

"That's good."

I really didn't know what else to say since I was sure at any moment he would be launching into his lecture of how I'd made his life a living hell and how much grief Dominick had given him after what I said.

"I wanted to come by and see how you're doing. You know, after the whole Alicia thing."

Even the allusion to her death made my eyes well with tears, but I held them back, not wanting to show Derek how much what had happened truly affected me. "I'm okay, but it only made me more resolute to bring the guilty man to justice."

For a moment, he remained still as a statue, but then he leaned toward me and said, "I promise you, Poppy, Jefferson Girard will pay for what he did to Geneva and Alicia. You have my word on it."

When he finished speaking, he turned his gaze toward the table where the former mayor and his wife sat and narrowed his eyes to angry slits. I watched as he stayed that way for nearly a minute before he turned toward me and smiled.

"Time for me to get back to my table. I'm happy you're okay, Poppy. Take care."

"Thanks, Derek."

He stood from the table and threw another nasty glare toward the mayor's table before turning to head back to where his party sat. I watched him walk past Girard and wondered if he'd say anything, but he simply kept moving until he reached his table.

And then as he pulled his chair out to sit, the light from the candle in the center of the table glinted off his handcuffs, and I suddenly felt like all the oxygen had been sucked out of the room.

Chapter Seventeen

"Excuse me, Miss McGuire, did you decide on what you'd like tonight?"

I looked up at the young man with the freshly scrubbed look standing next to my table and mumbled, "Nothing. I think I need to go. I'm sorry."

The waiter smiled meekly, clearly confused by my change of heart from just a few minutes earlier. "Okay. There's no check, so I hope you have a good night."

He walked away, and as I stood to leave, the fear that I wouldn't reach Alex in time raced through me. I hurried toward the door, but as I passed Derek's table, I felt his hand clap onto my forearm.

"Is something wrong, Poppy? You look like you've seen a ghost."

I looked down at where his hand held me and swallowed hard. "No, I'll be okay. I just heard from my father. He needs me, so I'm going across the street to help him."

Derek released his hold on me and smiled. "Maybe I'll stop in after dinner to say hi to him and see how he is. I haven't had a chance to stop in lately with this case taking up all my time."

"Yeah. I better go. See you later."

Tearing out of the restaurant, I ran at top speed to my house to get my car. Panting by the time I reached home, I jumped behind the wheel and started the car before I called Alex to let him know he'd been right all along.

His phone rang until it went to voicemail and I heard his steady voice instruct me to leave a message and he'd call me back when he could. At the beep, I began speaking, more like rambling, but then I stopped and calmly said, "Alex, I need you to call me back as soon as possible. It's a matter of life and death. Please call me back as soon as you get this message."

I stuck my phone in the cup holder next to my seat and put the car in gear. I couldn't wait around at my house for him to call me back. He had every right to still be angry with me, and if he was, he wouldn't be returning my call anytime soon. No, I had to go to him before it was too late.

Although I'd been known to put the pedal to the floor a few times in my life, never before had I driven as fast as I did getting to his house. I arrived to find it just like I had that first time I was there. Nearly all the rooms were dark, except for one toward the back. Instead of parking in the driveway this time, I drove a little ways further and found a spot hidden in between two tracts of trees about a hundred yards away from his house.

Doubling back, I reached his house and banged on the door, but he didn't answer. I pounded on his front door over and over, praying he'd hear the noise and open it, but nobody came. Adrenaline coursed through me at the thought that something had happened to him. Had the murderer gotten to him already?

I had to get his attention some way, so I crept

around the side of the house in the hopes that I might be able to see him through the window in that single lit room. I reached it and standing on my toes, I peered in. One light illuminated the room that looked like an office or a study, but no one sat at the desk or in either of the two leather wingback chairs. The real fear that Alex lay inside the house hurt or dead settled into my brain, and I knew I had to do something.

Ideas raced through my head. I could call him again and tell him I was right outside his house. No, he hadn't returned my call, so it was unlikely he'd answer another one. I could text him. Yes! If he was still safe inside and had his phone on him like he always did, he'd get the message that I was there so he could let me in.

I pulled my phone out of my pants' pocket and typed out a text, but when I pressed SEND, nothing happened. Looking up at the top of my phone screen, I saw I had no bars.

Damnit! I knew sticking with that small carrier would come back to haunt me someday. Why did it have to be at that very moment?

I had no choice but to go to drastic measures. I crouched down and rooted around on the ground for a rock big enough to smash through the window so either I could get his attention or I could get into the house to find him. Either would work. The problem was in the dark it was difficult to find much of anything, and all I kept picking up were tiny stones that wouldn't do the job.

Then I felt something that might work. A little heavier than I would have liked, I barely was able to lift the rock. Struggling to get to my feet with it in my hands, I turned around to hurl it at the glass and saw the red and blue lights of a police car coming down the road toward the house.

Had Alex called them thinking he had an intruder on his property? Dropping the oversized rock to the ground, I crept along the side of the house toward the front to watch and listen.

The car stopped in Alex's driveway behind his Mustang. Derek got out of the car and walked slowly up to the front door to knock on it. In the darkness, he examined the area and then took out his flashlight to shine it around him and I saw it wasn't Derek but Dominick.

Why would Dominick drive all the way out here instead of sending one of his officers?

As I hid in the darkness, I heard the front door open and Alex ask what was wrong as he turned on the front porch light. I heard in his voice the same confusion at seeing the chief of police of Sunset Ridge there at his door.

"Hi Alex. Is Poppy here?"

He hesitated for a moment and then answered, "No. I haven't seen her since yesterday."

"There's been another murder tonight. I'm worried she might be in danger."

"Another murder? You mean in addition to Alicia Jenkins?" Alex asked.

"Yes," Dominick said in a somber voice. "If you see her, call me. Her father would never forgive me if I let anything happen to her. Our families have been close since we were kids."

"I'll make sure to tell her if I see her."

I watched as Dominick returned to his police cruiser and drove away down the road. If I'd been afraid before, now I was terrified. Another murder? Who?

When his tail lights were no longer in sight, I bolted toward Alex's front door and once again banged on it desperately to get his attention. This time, thank God, he heard me.

The door opened and there he stood facing me for the first time since I'd said those horrible things. There wasn't a lot of time for me to apologize, but he had every right not to want to speak to me until I did, so I said what needed to be said.

Looking at those brown eyes that had been so full of hurt when I stormed out the last time, I saw some of that pain still lingered as he looked out at me. Hating that I had been the cause of that in him, I said, "I'm sorry for what I said, Alex. I had no right, and I'm so sorry for being that person."

He stared at me for what seemed like forever before he nodded. "You're not that person, Poppy. Come in."

I stepped inside the room that unfortunately held that one terrible memory for me and hoped this time would be different. Alex closed the door and said, "Maybe I should have handled things differently. I'm not the type of person to get all excited about a case, but I know you are. Maybe if I'd remembered that…"

"I know I jump to conclusions and that's not what a good detective does. I'm new at this, so I'm going to make mistakes. I know now the mayor isn't the killer."

The thought of yet another person dead because of my interference crushed me, and I hung my head. "I just wish I'd known in time before Alicia and now this new victim paid with their lives."

Alex gently put his arm around my shoulders. "Alicia's death isn't your fault, Poppy, and there is no new victim. Dominick lied."

I turned to face him and saw he was telling the truth. "What? Are you sure?"

"I've had the police scanner on all night, and there's been no mention of any new murder. He lied."

"Oh, my God! Why?"

Alex nodded. "I don't know, but I have my suspicions."

"Please don't do that thing you do with making me wait to find out what you're thinking. I don't think I can handle it now."

He took a deep breath and let it out before he spoke. "I think one of the Hampton brothers is the murderer."

The news that Alex thought one of the two people I'd known practically all my life was a murderer made my head spin. The excitement of the night also made me lightheaded all of a sudden, and I stumbled toward the couch to sit down.

"Are you okay? Did something happen to make you come out here?"

I got my bearings back and took a deep breath, only now realizing how close I came to being in danger. "Yeah. I went back to Diamanti's tonight because I was still convinced Jefferson Girard had killed Geneva and then Alicia because she was about to tell me who the mystery man going into Geneva's house was. He and his wife were there, and I took my spot at a table near them to watch what they did. That's when Derek joined me."

"What did he say?"

I hung my head and admitted the sad truth. "Nothing bad. I just can't believe it was one of them, Alex."

"You had the clue that made me realize it could be

right in your hand."

Now I was really confused. "What do you mean?"

He handed me the letter I'd received about Candy Skerrit at my office. "I thought about what you said about the handwriting and then tonight when I stopped in to see Derek at his office just as he was leaving I saw the same handwriting on note right on his desk."

"So was it Derek who did it and Dominick who tried to throw us off the scent or vice versa?"

Alex shook his head. "I don't know yet, and I'm not just making you wait to know what I think."

"I must have seen both of their handwriting dozens of times in my life. How could I have been so stupid not to notice?"

He sat down next to me and said in his nicest voice, "You weren't stupid. You just let the personalities of those involved in this case get in your way. That's all I meant when I said you were too close to the case."

"So Alicia's death is my fault. If I'd been any good at this whole solving crimes thing, I wouldn't have gotten her killed because I would have known who the murderer was."

"Alicia's death isn't your fault, Poppy. You didn't kill her."

I buried my face in my hands and closed my eyes. "I feel so terrible about what happened. First I was awful to you, and then one of them killed her. Why?"

"Because the murderer thought she knew what he'd done. He had the perfect way to manipulate her into letting him in the house, and then he did what he had to so his crime could remain a secret."

"If I'd been any good, I would have been onto him days ago. I didn't know until I saw Derek tonight, though. I watched him walk back to his table at Diamanti's and when he went to sit down, the light of the candle on his table hit his handcuffs and all of a sudden what Shelley said about seeing a glint of silver in the light came flooding back into my mind."

Alex patted my leg. "So which one is it? Derek, the charming guy everyone loves but nobody respects, or Dominick, the chief of police and hater of you poking your nose around in his police cases?"

At that moment, I wasn't anywhere close to being sure, but I knew Alex was. "Dominick?"

Nodding, Alex sighed. "Yeah. That handwriting is his. I snuck a look at something he signed on my way out of the police station tonight and saw it was the same as the note he wrote his brother and what you called the male handwriting on the note pointing us to Candy Skerrit. He tried to make it look like someone else's writing, but he didn't do a very good job. But who would ever think the chief of police would be a killer?

"I should have known something was wrong when he didn't immediately ream me out when he found out I was working on this case. That was so out of character for him it should have been a huge red flag. A neon red light pointing an arrow at his head."

"You're being too hard on yourself. For what it's worth, I want you to know you weren't entirely wrong about the connection between Jefferson Girard and Geneva Woodward."

I lifted my head and stared at him, curious to know how I wasn't wrong. "Really? How do you know?"

"After you left, I did a little digging for myself and even drove up to Vermont to that little town where they'd first met. Everyone involved in that love triangle and the missing woman is dead, except for Jonas, who is now the former mayor, so the truth is finally out. I spoke to the police up there and found out it wasn't Geneva who was having the affair with him. It was her twin sister, Genessa."

Now I was confused. "So who was found dead? Or was the article wrong?"

"Genessa. Want to guess who her murderer was?"

Smiling, I said, "Well, I think I'm going to fall back on my favorite suspect and say Jonas who is now Jefferson Girard."

Alex shook his head and chuckled. "No. Geneva herself. It seems Geneva was having an affair with her sister's husband while Genessa was having her own affair, and when she found out about Geneva, she confronted her. They fought, and Geneva pushed her sister down the grand staircase in the Woodward mansion in town. Because they were so wealthy and influential, the family covered it up by making poor Jonas a scapegoat and paying him off to leave town."

"Wow, and there I was accusing him of killing yet another person."

"I wouldn't take it too much to heart. Girard has kept the family's secret all these years, so he's guilty of that, at least, in addition to his tax cheating. He isn't exactly a shining example of innocence."

Thinking back to what Jeannette McMurphy told me about Geneva's nasty visits to the mayor all the while he was in office, I finally understood why she may have hated him. "I guess we know why Geneva was always so difficult with the mayor. She knew he had the goods on her."

Alex added, "And he lived in mortal fear that she

might at any moment let the police in Vermont know where the supposed murderer of Genessa was and then everything he'd done to build a life here would be gone. Little did he know the truth had come out about her death years ago."

We sat there quietly before I asked the most important question. Turning to face Alex, I tucked my leg underneath me. "What are we going to do about Dominick?"

He took a deep breath and let it out slowly. "That's the question. As the chief of police, he's not exactly someone we can just accuse of murdering two women. The issue is complicated by the fact that Derek is his brother, so going to the police may be a problem. I'm going to have to find proof he's the murderer."

"Wait. What happened to we? Why can't we work on finding proof that he's the murderer?"

Alex grimaced and stood from the couch. Folding his arms, he shook his head. "I believe he already thinks you know something, Poppy. It would be too dangerous for you to work on this anymore."

I jumped to my feet, furious that he was cutting me out now that we were so close to solving this case. "No! How exactly does it make me any safer not working on the case? What am I going to do until you get him? Hide out in my house terrified that every time someone knocks on my door or every time I hear a strange noise that it's him come to get me?"

Alex's eyes filled with a look of concern. Gently, he touched my shoulder and said, "You can stay at your father's. You'll be safe there. I won't need long to get the proof. Now that I know he's the murderer, I know what I'm looking for."

I pushed his hand off my shoulder and set my feet to stand toe-to-toe with him. No way was I being sent off to my father's like some helpless little girl.

"You can't do this. I won't let you. It's not fair that I've worked on this all along and now when we're so close—you hear that? *We're so close.* Now that we're so close to getting Geneva's murder solved, you want to hide me away while you get to do all the real detective work."

"This isn't some TV show, Poppy. Dominick is a real murderer. It's dangerous for you to be involved in this anymore."

"Why would it be safer for me to hide out at my father's? You don't think Dominick the real murderer will get to me there? I'm not even sure my father owns a gun, for God's sake. What are we supposed to do if he comes after me? Throw bottles of booze at him? Maybe some shot glasses?"

Clearly frustrated, Alex shook his head. "Poppy, you're in danger. Why can't you see that?"

"If I'm in danger, then what better place could there be for me than by your side? You won't let me get hurt, and you're a former cop. I think that has to trump what my father has going on with no gun but a bar full of mixed drink ingredients."

He opened his mouth to recite another laundry list of reasons why my not working on the case anymore would be best, but from outside the flashing red and blue lights of a police car stopped him. Quickly, he said, "Listen to me. Go into the hallway and stay there."

I didn't give him any trouble and did as he ordered as he went to the kitchen to get his gun. At the first sound of someone knocking on the front door, he put his finger to his lips to tell me to keep quiet as he passed me on his way to answer it and undoubtedly come face to face again with the murderer.

The sound of the door opening made my blood run cold, and I held my breath as I listened for what would come next.

A voice said, "Alex, I need to see Poppy. Now."

And then I heard nothing but the sound of my heartbeat pounding in my ears and drowning out everything else.

Chapter Eighteen

ALEX SAID NOTHING for a long moment, but then finally answered, "She's not here, Derek. I haven't seen her since yesterday."

I waited for Derek to apologize and ask Alex to let him know if I showed up, but instead he said, "I know she's here, Alex. I saw her Jeep parked a few yards down the road. I need to speak to her."

"Is this a formal request to enter my house, Derek?"

Derek sighed loud enough for me to hear it in the hallway. I knew him well enough to understand that meant he was frustrated, but could we trust him? Was he involved in the murders with his brother?

I had a hard time believing that. As much as I had to admit I never dreamed Dominick would be a murderer, the idea that Derek would do anything to hurt another soul just seemed impossible. It wasn't who he was.

"Alex, it's one cop asking for help from another cop to keep someone we both care about safe. That's all this is."

I held my breath waiting to hear what Alex would do. Letting Derek in might be inviting in a man who wanted me dead, even if I couldn't believe that about him. As I thought about what would happen next, I heard Alex finally speak again.

"Come in, Derek."

Peeking around the hallway corner to see Alex backing up toward where I was, I rose to stand behind him. He shielded me with his body, protecting me from someone who'd been a friend of mine since when I wore Mary Janes and knee socks.

Derek's brown eyes opened wide in surprise. "I'm happy to see you here, Poppy. I was worried about you after you ran out of Diamanti's. Are you okay?"

Alex's body tensed up against mine, but he remained calm as he offered Derek a seat in the living room. "Let's sit down."

He stopped me when I took a step toward the couch and whispered, "Don't say a word about Dominick."

I nodded and followed him to where Derek sat waiting for us. Taking a seat next to Alex on the couch, I studied the face of the man who'd once been a sixth grade boy who told me he'd love me forever and hoped he wasn't a bad guy like his brother.

"Are you okay? Why'd you run out?" he asked, those familiar eyes filled with concern.

"I'm good. It was just the mention of Alicia that made me feel like I needed to get out of there."

"Dominick told me at dinner that you were with him when he found Alicia dead. He said you were pretty shaken up by what you saw."

Guilt over her death pinched at me, and I swallowed hard. "I wasn't shaken by seeing her lying there dead on her grandmother's floor. The fact that I was to blame for what happened to her was…"

I choked up, letting my sentence trail off. Thankfully, Alex took over and did the talking.

"I've told Poppy she's not to blame, and I'm sure you'll say the same. But she's having a hard time dealing with what happened."

Derek leaned forward toward me, and before my eyes, he morphed into that boy who'd professed his love for me on the way home from school that last day of the year. "Poppy, that wasn't your fault. You and Alicia were both in danger. I'm just glad you didn't get hurt."

"You do realize the same person who killed Geneva also killed Alicia, right?" Alex asked.

"We still don't know who the murderer of Geneva is. I've followed all the leads you two gave me, but neither Shelley nor Candy could have done it. The coroner says the marks on Geneva's neck show the killer had to be much stronger than either woman. He thinks it had to be a male."

"The mayor," I said quietly, hating that I had to lie to Derek. "It had to be Jefferson Girard."

"Do you know about the former mayor's history with Geneva?" Alex asked Derek, who immediately rolled his eyes.

"Know about it? I've had to listen to him complain about her and her visits to his office right up to election day when he was voted out. She was a thorn in his side, for sure. I don't know if it's enough to make him want to strangle her, though."

Alex reached over to the end table on his side of the couch to get the papers I'd left the day before. Handing them to Derek, he said, "There's a lot more to them than just once-a-week nuisance complaints by Geneva."

As Derek read over the papers I'd printed out and examined the pictures, Alex nudged my arm. I turned my head slightly and saw him give me a look I knew meant we were on the same page about leading Derek on a wild goose chase. I didn't like it, but letting him in on what we knew about his older brother was too risky.

"So that's why Dominick has been on the warpath about the mayor in the last two days," Derek mumbled. Holding the papers up, he asked, "Can I keep these?"

"Yes. I meant to give them to you right after I spoke to Alex about what's contained in them, but I didn't get the chance. I'm sorry, Derek. I wasn't trying to keep anything from you."

He smiled warmly, making me feel even worse about lying. "I would never think you'd keep something from me, Poppy. If I can't trust the first girl I said I love you to, then who can I trust?"

For a moment as the three of us sat talking about the murder of two women, a tiny bit of sweetness and light crept into our conversation. Alex smiled, and I saw that no matter what had happened, Derek was still that boy I'd known all my life.

"Well, I'm not entirely innocent," I joked while the truth of how duplicitous I actually was being with him made me hate what I had to do.

Derek blushed at my insinuation, but then he asked, "Dominick told me you were supposed to meet with Alicia. What were you going to talk about? Did it have to do with Geneva's murder?"

I felt Alex tense up again, likely worried that I'd forget not to say anything about Dominick as I explained all about what I believed Alicia was about to tell me that night. I wouldn't let him down, though.

"Alicia saw the man Shelley said had been visiting Geneva each night. This same man came to her house the night she was murdered. Alicia thought she knew who the man was. She didn't want to talk about it or say his name over the phone, so we agreed to meet at the Madison that night. She never showed, even though I waited over an hour, and by the time I got to her grandmother's house, she must have been dead."

Derek hung his head and blew the air out of his lungs slowly. "I wish she would have told me. I would have been able to help her."

I hated seeing the regret all over his face, so I quickly said, "I'm guessing she thought it was someone important in town that she didn't think you could have protected her from. I think she thought Geneva's mystery man who came to visit and then killed her that night was Jefferson Girard, and when he found out she was going to tell me, he killed her too."

Derek ran his hand through his hair in frustration. "Too bad I don't have a lick of evidence to prove that. I can't just haul the former mayor of our town in for questioning. As much as I hate to admit it, like I told Dominick when he demanded I do just that yesterday, we have to answer to the town council and even though Girard isn't mayor anymore, he's still got lots of friends on that council. I'll lose my job if this all turns out to be a dead end and the murderer is someone else."

"Well, now that we know who did it, we can dig for proof," Alex said in his best upbeat voice. "Girard isn't going anywhere anytime soon. We can bide our time and help you build an airtight case."

"That's all well and good, Alex, but who's going to make sure Poppy's safe?"

I suddenly felt like some helpless girl in those blue knee socks from elementary school again. I didn't need people to keep me safe. Not from the former mayor and not from Dominick.

"Please stop talking about me like I'm invisible or inconsequential. I'm right here."

Both Derek and Alex turned to look at me with surprise on their faces. "Poppy, this is serious. I was fine with you helping with the case, but that was before a second murder occurred. I'd never forgive myself if something happened to you."

Rolling my eyes, I said, "Thank you, but I'm not some damsel in distress, Derek, and Alex can help make sure the mayor doesn't get anywhere near me."

"You're okay with this, Alex?"

I looked at Alex and wondered why Derek would think he wouldn't be okay with it. He'd offered before, so what could be the issue?

But Alex simply nodded. "Of course."

Derek still looked unsure about Alex keeping me safe, but he didn't pursue the issue, even though I now wanted to know why he hadn't thought he'd want the job of keeping me safe.

"Okay. I want to catch up with you two tomorrow after I do some digging on the former mayor, and as always, I want to know everything you find out. Agreed?"

Alex and I promised to share anything we found out about Jefferson Girard, and as Derek walked toward the front door, he turned to look at me and smiled. "I don't want to lose my first love, okay? Don't do anything stupid and listen to Alex."

"I'm not really good at listening," I joked. But seeing the look of concern in his eyes, I stopped my kidding. "Don't worry, Derek. Things are going to be okay. You're a good guy. Don't worry. When this is all over, the three of us will get a drink at my dad's bar and maybe laugh about things."

"Maybe I'll be able to convince Dominick to join us since he's had an ax to grind against Jefferson Girard for a while, and I think he'll be up for celebrating the end of this case."

I hoped my uneasiness at hearing Dominick's name didn't show all over my face. I hated thinking how hard Derek would take hearing what his brother had done. Ever since we were all children, he'd looked up to him. Three years older, Dominick had always been everything Derek wanted to be. When he captained the football team in his senior year, all Derek could talk about was how he'd do the same when he got to his senior year. And when he did, it was Dominick's return home from school to see that first game of the season that thrilled his younger brother more than anything that year.

Now Derek would have to accept the fact that the person he'd based his entire life on was exactly the type of person he'd taken an oath to protect people from. I didn't know how he'd deal with it.

"Maybe," I squeaked out, sad for what the future held for my friend and the first boy to ever like me.

Alex stood to follow Derek to the door. "I'm wondering if we should keep Poppy's involvement with the case out of any discussions with the chief. He seemed quite worried about her when he came by before."

"Dominick was here tonight?"

"Yeah. A short time before you came. I just wonder if it might be more helpful to keep her part in this quiet."

Derek didn't respond, but the way he looked at me and then at Alex like suddenly he was more troubled than before made me feel like he knew what we thought his brother had done. I didn't know why, but it was just a vibe I had.

"We'll get together with you tomorrow," I said, still not sure how long Alex and I would be able to keep up the charade that Jefferson Girard was our suspect.

He smiled and nodded before turning to Alex and saying in a low voice I barely heard, "Be careful tonight. If Girard is the killer, he's got nothing to lose coming out here to get her. He's a man with a lot of power who believes he's above the law."

After he left, Alex walked back to where I sat and I couldn't help see how Derek had described the former mayor could just as well apply to his own brother. The police chief of Sunset Ridge had as much or more power than any mayor of the town, and I'd long wondered if the quarrel between Dominick and Jefferson Girard wasn't more about two men jockeying for power than it was about justice and upholding the law.

"He's going to take it hard when he finds out his brother is the killer," Alex said quietly.

"I know. He's admired him so much he put him on a pedestal. I don't know how he's going to handle news like that."

Alex leaned back away from me and smiled. "It sounds like he has someone else up on a pedestal."

I waved away his insinuation that Derek Hampton had any real feelings for me. "Don't be ridiculous. Derek and I are friends. Period."

Shrugging, he said, "I don't know. You were the first girl he ever said I love you to. That sounds pretty serious, Poppy."

His teasing lightened my mood a little, and I

couldn't help but smile at the idea that what a boy said to me twenty years ago meant anything.

"I'm sure he's said those words to a lot of women since then. Derek is the most popular single guy in town, maybe even the county. Well, at least he was until you showed up in Sunset Ridge."

Now it was Alex's turn to roll his eyes. "I think his place as number one bachelor around here is pretty safe. I don't think he has anything to worry about."

"For now, maybe, but from the way Jennie at The Grounds was talking, your calendar might get very full very soon."

His smile faded into a frown, and he stood from the couch. Looking down at me, he said, "I'm not interested in anything like that."

I didn't say anything in return because clearly the time for joking had ended. He walked away into the kitchen and left me sitting there unsure what had happened to change his mood so suddenly.

Then he spoke again and whatever he'd been unhappy about was gone. "Do you want something to drink? I have beer and some vodka."

I stood to follow him into the kitchen confused that he hadn't mentioned his favorite drink. I was sure I'd been right in thinking I at least knew that about him. "No scotch? I thought that was your drink of choice."

He turned away from the island in the center of the kitchen to get glasses from the cabinet. "No. I never keep scotch here at the house."

"Why? If it's your favorite, why only drink it when you're out?"

Placing two beer glasses on the island, he said, "Beer it is then since you didn't say otherwise."

Something in the way he sidestepped a very simple question made me want to know the answer even more, but everything about his body language and stern facial expression as he poured my drink told me ignorance might be bliss in this case. He handed me my glass and raised his in the air.

"To solving our first case together."

I raised mine to share his toast and said, "We haven't really solved it yet, though. Dominick is still walking the streets free, and we don't have enough proof that he's the killer to even be able to accuse him."

He took a sip of his beer and smiled. "True, but we will so I didn't think it was too early to raise a glass to our success."

"What do you think we'll need to find to make an airtight case against him?"

"We'll need to pin Shelley down on Dominick being Geneva's mystery man. I also think we can find evidence of his relationship with her in that house. Now that we know they were together, I think it will be pretty easy. Something tells me he didn't pay attention to being invisible there until the night he murdered her."

"I still can't really get my head around it. Why kill her? It's not like them being together had to be some state secret. They were both single adults, so why do the sneaking in the back door routine in the middle of the night?"

A noise at the back of the house startled us out of our discussion about the case, and Alex immediately moved to check it out. "I'll be right back. I put my gun back on the bottom shelf in the island if I tell you to bring it to me."

I watched as he disappeared down the hallway. The

wind had begun to pick up earlier, so the noise was likely just a branch knocking against a window. I took a sip of my beer and from behind me I heard a knock at the front door.

"Poppy, it's Derek."

Hurrying to the door, I yelled to Alex, "Derek's back, so hang on. I'll send him around to see what the noise was on the outside."

I opened the door just as I heard Alex yell something, and then before I knew it there was Dominick's face glaring at me as he pushed hard on the door. I tried to close it, but it was no use. He was far too strong, and in just seconds, he charged through the door, overpowering me as he took hold of me.

It all happened so fast that before I knew it, the one person who wanted me dead had me in his hold as Alex ran into the room with a horrified look on his face. I'd foolishly fell for the trick Dominick and Derek had played on me countless times growing up, and now I'd pay the ultimate price for it.

Chapter Nineteen

D OMINICK HELD ME tightly, crushing me in his arms as he breathed heavily next to my ear and pressed his gun into my right ribs. I'd seen him rejoice in the end zone after he threw the winning touchdown in the state playoff game and cry like a baby at his father's funeral a year later. I'd watched him punish bullies who'd been picking on Derek on the way home from school and stand proudly smiling with an ear to ear grin in front of the police station the day he was promoted to chief.

But I'd never seen Dominick Hampton like he looked as he came through that door at me. The rage in his eyes and the twisted look of madness on his face terrified me. Whoever he'd been all those times I considered him a friend, he wasn't that person anymore.

In my ear, he whispered low and ominous, "Always so trusting, Poppy. You're such a small town girl, aren't you? Didn't you ever think it might be me, or did you naturally assume it was that lovesick brother of mine coming back to tell you how worried he is about you again?"

I looked over at Alex as he stood frozen at the end of the hallway. He took a step toward the kitchen where I knew his gun sat in the island just feet away, but

Dominick reacted immediately.

"Take another step and Poppy gets a bullet in her."

Alex stopped dead and turned back to face us. He raised his hands in surrender and calmly tried to speak to Dominick. "Okay, okay. This doesn't have to go down this way. Just let her go and whatever happened we can figure it out."

Behind me, Dominick pushed the gun hard against my side. "Poppy, your friend seems to think I'm one of the pieces of shit he's used to dealing with in the big city. Tell him how much this gun pressing into your ribs hurts so maybe he'll understand he needs to talk to me as his equal."

My side felt like at any moment the metal of the gun would break through my ribcage and send pieces of bone scattering inside my body. Tears welled in my eyes as I pleaded with Alex, "Do as he says, please. He's the police chief of Sunset Ridge."

"Okay, I'm sorry, Dominick. You're right."

"I knew from the moment you moved here you'd be a problem. Then when it seemed like you were busy hiding out away from the world out here, I thought things would be okay. You see, Derek and the rest of my guys would never think for a second that I was up to something all those nights I was supposed to be on duty but I was nowhere to be found."

Alex nodded. "When you were at Geneva's, right?"

A low chuckle erupted from Dominick's throat. "It's not what you think, big city cop. I'm guessing you and Nancy Drew here think I killed her because we were sleeping together."

"That's not why you strangled her?" Alex asked, clearly as confused as I was at hearing Geneva's death hadn't been a crime of passion.

"No. Geneva got what she deserved because she was planning to do to me what she'd done to that idiot Jefferson Girard. Like I could ever be manipulated like that local yokel political clown."

Not understanding what he meant, I stupidly asked, "What are you talking about? Do you mean the business in Vermont?"

He laughed again and pulled me tighter into him. "You are too clever for your own good sometimes, Poppy. You know that? But this time you only knew half the story. Too bad you'll never know the whole story."

Alex's eyes flashed fear for the first time since I'd known him and when he spoke, I knew he was struggling to keep calm. He didn't sound like he always had when he spoke to me. There was a shakiness to his voice now.

"You don't have to do this, Dominick. There's no point in killing her. Don't...don't do this."

Dominick said nothing to Alex's suggestion, and then just when I thought all was lost, he pushed me hard toward my partner so I stumbled into his arms. Thinking he'd just made a huge mistake, I hurried to stand only to find Dominick's gun now pointed right at Alex's head.

"Stay right where you are, big city. You're right. There is a point in killing you, though. As popular as our little friend here is in Sunset Ridge, I doubt many people will believe her if she tries to say I held the two of you at gunpoint before putting a bullet in your head. You, on the other hand, your word might carry more weight."

I looked down at Alex and then back up at Dominick. "Nobody knows him in town, and they'd believe him before they'd believe me? Why?"

"Now's not really the time, Poppy," Alex said in a

tone that was a mix of fear and frustration.

"Yes, it is," I said as I looked down at him again and gave him a wink. What I was doing was a huge gamble, but when a crazy man had a gun at my partner's head, all bets were off as to what would work to get us out of the situation.

"Listen to him, Poppy. Now's not the time."

I winked at Alex again and lifted my head to face Dominick. If I could buy us some time, maybe by some divine intervention or miracle, Derek would come back and find us being held by his brother.

On the other hand, I might just anger the guy with the gun pointed at Alex. I couldn't think like that now, though.

"I want to know why anyone in Sunset Ridge would believe him over me. For God's sake, I've lived here all my life. My family's lived here for years. I write for the town's newspaper, and you say the people in this town will believe him before me?"

Dominick's eyebrows shot up as he looked at me in confusion. "You aren't really like the rest of us, Poppy. You're already in your thirties, you've never been married, and you work for some two-bit version of Entertainment Tonight, so people think you're a little weird."

I didn't know which of those statements bothered me more—the slam about me being an unmarried woman in her early thirties or the implication that being gainfully employed, even if it was at a lame job, was a reason not to believe me.

"You're older than I am, and you aren't married. Why does my not having a husband make me less credible?"

"I guess you should have jumped on the chance to hook up with my brother way back when," he said with a grin.

"And as for my job at The Bottom Line, that should make me more believable, not less," I argued, caught up in the moment and forgetting for a second that Dominick could pull the trigger anytime.

"That's your problem, Poppy. You're always wanting to stick your nose in places where it doesn't belong. Give a girl a college degree and she thinks she can do better than the police can."

"So that's your problem with me? I'm smart and you feel inferior because of that?"

Alex nudged my leg. "Now is not the time for this, Poppy."

I looked down and saw by the fear in his eyes he didn't have a whole lot of confidence in my tactics. He had every right to worry, but I had to try something to keep Dominick from going through with killing both of us, and the one thing I knew about the Hampton brothers was they loved to talk.

"Listen to him, Poppy. I have a gun pointed at his head. He understands what that means."

"Well, if you're just going to shoot the two of us, at least explain why you did what you did. Why did you kill Geneva?"

Slowly, his expression softened and a big smile spread across his face. "So that's how you want to do it? Like they do in movies? Okay, Poppy. For old time's sake since our families have been close for years, I'll tell you why. And then I'm going to kill you both."

My heart clenched as he mentioned the closeness of our families. My father had no one else but me, and now

Dominick wanted to take that away from him, someone who'd closed his bar during the football season and stood on the sidelines every Friday night to cheer him and Derek on.

Well, if he thought I was just going to give in and be taken away from my father that easily, he had another thing coming. I didn't know how, but I was going to get out of this alive, and I was going to be joined by Alex too.

"Well, I'm all ears, as I'm sure my partner is. Tell us what we couldn't figure out."

Dominick took a small step back while still keeping his gun pointed at Alex's head and began his story. "You thought Geneva died because of some romantic thing between us, but that was just the tip of the iceberg. Yeah, she and I were sleeping together, but we'd been doing that for years. We kept it pretty well hidden by meeting at a hotel in the next county, but then Geneva began insisting we meet at her house instead."

"Why? If you two didn't want anyone to know, why take the chance that someone would see you?" Alex asked.

Looking down at him, Dominick nodded. "See? This is a how men think. Females focus on nonsense like them not having the right lighting for doing their makeup at the hotel. I swear to God I wanted to kill her so many times when she was whining about that crap."

"Sounds like a match made in heaven," I sniped.

Dominick waved his gun toward Alex. "See? You know what I had to deal with. She's the same way."

"Well, it's our cross to bear," Alex said somberly.

Was he serious? I certainly hoped he was just playing along because if he wasn't, I'd have something to say about it once we got out of this situation.

"Can we get back to why you killed her and stop bashing on women for a moment?"

Both men looked at me like I'd broken some unwritten rule, and I wondered if I'd pushed Dominick too far for once.

"I was only speaking the truth. Geneva demanded we begin meeting at her house about four months ago, so since I really didn't want to give up a good thing, if you know what I mean, I said okay, and we moved from a couple times a week at the hotel to a couple times a week at her house. Same time as always. Right around midnight."

"But this wasn't just sex between you two, you said. Right?" I asked, still completely in the dark about what else Dominick and Geneva were doing together.

"No. Sex was a nice benefit, but what we were doing was something even better. Geneva was blackmailing that dopey Jefferson Girard and we were sharing in the gains."

"Blackmailing him? About what? That thing in Vermont?" I asked.

A low chuckle like a rumble exploded out of Dominick's mouth and he threw his head back for just a moment before he caught himself and refocused on Alex and me. "No. That was nothing compared to what Girard was up to when he was in office. That thief stole hundreds of thousands of dollars from the town, and our stupid council couldn't figure out what was going on. We knew it was no use to tell them, so we took advantage of a situation and made a ton of green from that stooge."

From below me, I heard Alex ask, "Then why kill your partner in crime? The two of you were making money, so why stop now?"

"I never wanted to stop, but leave to Geneva to ruin a perfectly good thing. I got to her house that night ready to hear how her last meeting went with Girard. Ever since he left office, she'd been having him meet her across town near Candy's. She'd met with him to get another payment, but she didn't want to talk about that. All she wanted to talk about was how unfair our agreement was. Like our sixty/forty agreement wasn't good enough. I was the one who found out about his stealing. All she did was hold that damn thing in Vermont over his head."

"He didn't even kill her sister. Did you know that?" I asked.

He sneered and shot me a look of disgust. "Yeah. She did that to her own sister. If Girard wasn't guilty of other things, he probably would have stood up to her and stopped everything we were doing. He had too much to hide, though, so we took advantage of that. Not that Geneva did much other than harp on him. I did all the work finding out what he'd been up to."

Dominick stopped for a moment and then sighed. "I didn't go there planning to kill her that night. I just wanted to enjoy a night with her like we always did. Why couldn't she just be happy with that? Why did she have to get greedy?"

"That's the kind of person she was, Dominick," I said, not so much supporting him as trying to keep him talking by explaining the reality of who Geneva really was. "She walked around town lording her wealth over everyone all the time. It's why she was hated by so many people."

He sighed again, this time even deeper. "Yeah. If

only she could have been happy with the forty percent she was getting. I wasn't cheating her out of anything she deserved."

"Did she threaten to tell someone if you didn't agree?" Alex asked as I sensed Dominick was beginning to crack under the strain of telling us what had happened.

Shoulders sagging, he nodded. "Yeah. I got there and she launched into me immediately. Not even a hello kiss. No, she wanted to know why she was getting so much less even though she had to do all the work. I tried to calm her down. I took her in my arms like always and kissed her, but she wouldn't stop talking about how she deserved at least a fifty/fifty split or more."

He shook his head and frowned. Looking down at Alex, I searched his eyes for any sign he knew how to get us out of this since I'd kept Dominick talking all this time to no avail. Derek hadn't returned, and it didn't look like he would in time to save us from what his brother had planned.

"If it was an accident, maybe the district attorney won't press murder charges," Alex suggested.

Dominick's frown grew deeper. "No, it was murder. She wouldn't stop. She pushed me away and poked me over and over in the chest while she harped on about wanting more and how she held my career in her hands. And then something inside me snapped. I spun her around and with that scarf she had hung around her neck, I choked her. She stopped talking, but her arms flailed all over the place as she fought me. It was no use. And then before I knew it, she was dead weight in my arms and I let her go and she slid down onto the floor."

"Did you take her rings?" I asked, baffled why he

would since he hadn't gone there to rob her.

Dominick grimaced. "I always hated those rings. Do you know how many times she smacked me in the face with them? Talk about killing the mood. She owed me for all the grief she'd caused me, so yeah, I took them."

"How did you find out Alicia Jenkins was going to talk to me? I didn't tell anyone."

"I'd seen you following Girard and wanted to see what you knew. I saw you go to her grandmother's house and figured it wasn't her who would have seen me going into Geneva's. But Alicia was a different story. I waited for her to come home, knowing her grandmother had already gone upstairs after I saw the lights go on up on the second floor, and I knew as soon as I saw Alicia that she'd seen me that night."

"I thought she was going to tell me it was the mayor who she saw that night going into Geneva's," I said in a low voice, feeling the guilt over Alicia's death press on me again.

"If only you hadn't poked your nose around in things that were none of your business. I've been telling you that for years, Poppy, but you never listen and my brother lets you get involved even though I forbid him too. It's going to break his heart when you're gone. For that, I do feel bad."

"Well, thanks, Dominick. But why not just let us live? You can take your money you got from the mayor and go anywhere you want. Alex and I swear we won't tell a soul about this."

Dominick grinned and shook his head. "Not going to happen, Poppy, but nice try. No, this is where it ends for you and your cop friend. It's too bad that you didn't listen, but then again, you never have been the type to do as you're told. Maybe if you had…"

Behind him, the door suddenly flew open and there stood Derek with his gun pointed directly at his brother. "Put the gun down and back away from them, Dom!"

Stunned for just a moment at how quickly things had changed, Dominick turned around and laughed. "Go home, Derek. We'll talk when I get done here. Don't do anything stupid. I don't want you to get hurt when you don't have to."

Alex scrambled to his feet and ran into the kitchen as I followed him and ducked behind the island. Grabbing his gun, he pointed it at Dominick as the two brothers stood facing off against one another.

"You killed two people, big brother. I can't let you kill anyone else. Don't do this and force me to do something I don't want to do."

"You won't do anything, Derek. The only reason you got to be a cop in this town is because of me. Without my help, you'd still just be a wannabe, and wannabes don't pull it out in clutch situations. Go home before you get hurt."

Dominick turned to face us and pointed the gun directly at me. "First you, and then him. I'll make it look like a murder-suicide by an unstable man who's never recovered from the death of his wife years before. Yeah, I know all about you, big city cop. Derek told me everything. Nobody will question the chief of police and I'll get away scot-free."

What happened next felt like the world had changed to slow motion speed. Derek yelled for him to put down his gun, and then all I heard were shots. I fell to the ground and covered my head until the horrible noise of bullets exploding out of the guns stopped. Next to me, I saw Alex standing there with his gun still pointing toward Dominick.

"What happened?" I asked, terrified if I looked toward the living room that I'd see both Hampton brothers shot.

"Are you okay, Poppy?" Alex asked as he helped me to my feet.

"Yeah, I'm okay. What about you?"

Alex nodded. "I'm fine."

Sadness gripped my heart at my next question. "What about them?"

He looked over at where they'd stood just a minute before, and I followed his gaze to see Derek crouched next to his brother on the floor. "We both shot at the same time, so I don't know who got him," he said quietly.

I ran over to where Dominick lay bleeding from his chest and hated the look of pure anguish I saw on Derek's face. "Is he going to be okay?"

Shaking his head, Derek struggled to hold back his tears. "No."

Dominick's eyes fixed on his brother as he tried to speak one last time, but it was no use. He took his final breath and then without another sound left us. Derek gently closed those eyes that looked so much like his and hung his head.

"I so wanted to be wrong about what I thought."

I put my arm around his shoulder and squeezed him to me. "Thank you for saving us. I didn't know if you'd come back, but I had to hope you would."

"After the computer tech guy at the station told me the reports had been tampered with, I had him do a complete check of the records. He called me when I got back to my office and told me dozens of calls had been deleted from the system. I called Dominick and saw his phone's GPS said he was back here, and I knew something was wrong. Too much didn't make sense unless it was him behind Alicia's murder, and that only happened because he needed to keep her quiet about whatever she knew he'd done."

Alex touched my shoulder and I saw the sadness in his eyes. Neither one of us had wanted things with Dominick to end like this.

"Are you two going to be okay? It's hard to lose someone you love, and I know you cared for him too, Poppy."

"Yeah," I said as I gave Derek's shoulder another squeeze. "We Sunset Ridge people are tough."

I looked back at the man lying on the ground in a pool of blood and decided I didn't want to think of Dominick Hampton that way for the rest of my life. I wanted to remember him as that teenage boy who stood up to those bullies giving his brother and me a hard time.

To remember him as the good guy we'd always thought he was.

Chapter Twenty

THREE DAYS LATER, I sat in my comfy chair with a book still recovering from my first time being involved in a shooting. Movies and television had always made it look like seeing someone shot wasn't a big deal, but in person, the entire thing shook me to my core. One minute Dominick was standing right in front of me breathing and talking, and then the next, he was gone and all that was left of him were our memories.

I hadn't cried yet, even after three whole days, but I knew it would come eventually. I'd known him my entire life, and now he wasn't in the world anymore. No matter what he turned out to be, it still pressed on my heart that he wouldn't be chastising me for sticking my nose into his police business ever again.

Like a weight on my shoulders pushing them down, the memory of him lying there and still looking up at his brother in surprise that he'd actually had the strength to shoot him stayed fixed in my mind. I imagined it would for a long time.

So much of this case had been life changing. Dominick lost his life. Derek lost his brother. Alicia lost her life. I still felt to blame for that. I always would.

Other changes had happened too. For the first time

since my mother died, I'd had to face death. And like with my mother, I still hated it. I hated it for how terrified it made me. I hated it for how weak it made me feel. But most of all, I hated how I couldn't control anything about it. Watching Dominick die had proven that to me.

Then there was the biggest change of all. Alex. In such a short time, I'd grown closer to him than I had to anyone ever in my life other than my parents. When I saw that gun pointed at his head, a mix of feelings rushed over me. I was angry and scared Dominick might kill him, but there were other emotions coursing through me too.

Genuine sadness at the possibility that he might not be in my life anymore. A desire to save him like he'd been so willing to do for me.

Did I care for him more than a friend and partner? I closed my eyes as the question tumbled around in my brain. I didn't know the answer. All I knew was the mere thought of losing him had affected me so much that I doubted I'd have been able to handle it if it was him lying there in a pool of blood dying in front of me instead of Dominick.

There were a million reasons for me not to feel more than friendship for him. At the very top of the list was the real fact he was in love with a ghost. I didn't know the whole story about his late wife, but Dominick had mentioned it as a reason why people would believe our deaths could be attributed to a murder-suicide so I had to believe I wasn't wrong about him still being in love with her all these years later.

Alex had alluded to how he'd retreated from the world when he came to Sunset Ridge when he first offered to help me on Geneva's case. Return to the land of the living was how he put it. Had he hidden away for all those years since his wife died?

Even more, was he anywhere near ready to actually be anyone but the man who lost her?

As I sat there curled up with my favorite blanket, my knees pulled up to my chest as I had for much of the last three days, I didn't know what I should feel about him. I'd never met any man like him. That I knew. He saw things I worried I'd never see, no matter how much time I spent around him. Whatever he had that made him see them, I wanted to learn that.

More than admiration for his detective skills, though, did I feel something else for him even I didn't want to admit?

Just as important, did he feel anything for me? I didn't know. He'd never shown he felt much of anything for anyone, but that was who he was. That was Alex. Did his stony exterior hide feelings that had grown inside him for me? Was he even capable of that since he still mourned his wife?

Thinking about all of this made me less sure than ever about my life. I'd never truly known what my path was. For so long, I'd been asking questions, first about why my mother had to die and then about the behavior of the famous people I researched. Was my true calling working with Alex solving crimes?

I had no inkling if he even wanted to continue doing that with me. We hadn't spoken since he followed me home that night to make sure I was okay. Driving right behind me all the way here, he walked with me to my door and came in to check everything was as it should be because he said I looked shaken up.

Then he told me if I needed anything I should call him and left. Part of me felt selfish for not offering him the same thing. He'd shot a man, and even though it hadn't been Alex's bullet that killed Dominick, he must have felt something about it. The problem was I didn't know what to say. I was too confused and sad.

So I didn't offer, even though later I wondered if I should call him and do just that. I didn't. Unlike most times in my life, I feared saying the wrong thing, so I said nothing.

I grabbed my phone off the side table next to my chair and checked for any messages from him, but there were none. All I saw were the handful from Bethany asking if I needed anything and to let her know when I wanted to talk and the one from my boss at The Bottom Line letting me know as much as he hated to do it, he had to fire me for not getting my piece completed on time days ago.

A tiny part of me regretted letting him down but not enough to make me plead for my job back. I felt bad disappointing him because he'd been a great boss and had given me a chance at my first real investigative reporter job, and for that, I'd always be thankful.

It just felt like it was time to leave that part of my life, though.

Not since my mother died had I felt at such loose ends. I didn't answer Bethany because I didn't know what I needed. One minute I wanted to run away from Sunset Ridge and never look back, and then the next minute I couldn't imagine leaving my house and the security it promised.

My phone rang with the day's fourth call from my father. Answering it, I said, "Hi, Dad. What's new?"

"I just wanted to check on you, Poppy. How are you doing?"

I couldn't help but smile at his question. That was the twelfth time he'd asked me that since that night, and I had the distinct feeling my answer every time was a bit lacking.

"I'm fine, Dad. How are you?"

"Will you be coming to the bar tonight? I can make my world famous beef stew I know you always love and we can sit and talk."

I wished I could say yes. I knew it would make him feel better if I did, but I just wasn't ready to leave this room and this comfy chair yet. "Not tonight, Dad. Maybe tomorrow."

He remained silent, likely disappointed by my turning him down again, and then asked as he had all those times before, "Is there anything you need, sweetheart? I'm just a phone call away. Don't forget that."

"I won't, Dad. I don't need anything right now, but thanks. I'll talk to you tomorrow, okay?"

"Okay. Poppy, remember I'm here if you need to talk."

"Thanks, Dad. Talk to you tomorrow."

I pressed END and let the phone drop into the blanket. I truly wished I knew what to say to him to explain that I wasn't depressed or anything like that. I didn't know what I was, to be honest. Mostly, I just felt lost. I didn't know if that was from seeing someone die again like I had with my mother or if it was something altogether different.

All I knew was there wasn't anywhere else in the world I wanted to be at that moment than right there under a blanket in my living room chair with the puffy cushions that enveloped me every time I sat down.

I didn't know how long I sat there with my eyes closed, unsuccessfully trying to push the memory of Dominick dead at my feet out of my brain. When I finally opened them to see who was knocking at my door, it was already dark out and I'd spent another entire day curled up in my living room.

The knocking became more insistent, so I trudged off to answer the door, not even caring that I was still wearing my Scottie dog black and red pajamas I'd worn for days. I didn't exactly look like I should to entertain guests, but it wasn't like I'd invited whoever it was who kept knocking.

I threw the door open and there stood Alex. Whatever he was feeling about Dominick's death, it didn't show on the outside. Dressed in jeans and a black sweater, he looked the picture of happiness.

Well, as much as he ever did.

His eyes scanned me from head to toe and then his gaze settled on my face, which was unwashed for the day and without a stitch of makeup.

"Can I come in?"

Nodding, I stepped back to let him into my kitchen. "Sure. Come on in."

I closed the door and turned to see him standing there awkwardly in the center of the room, as if he had come by to talk about something uncomfortable. Or maybe it was just his reaction to seeing me like this.

"I wanted to check to make sure you're okay," he said in a gentle tone like social workers use on people so they don't upset them.

"I'm fine. You don't have to worry about me." I

brushed past him on my way to the refrigerator and asked, "Would you like something to drink? I think the milk might still be good, and there's always diet soda in here."

I didn't know why, but as I stared in my nearly empty refrigerator, the tears began to well up in my eyes. Diet soda and milk being my only beverage choices really was no reason to begin sobbing like a baby, so I willed the tears away before I turned around to see him staring at me.

"Poppy, it's okay to be upset about what happened."

Waving him off, I shrugged my shoulders. "I'm not upset. I'm okay. Neither of those drinks sound any good?"

He frowned and shook his head. "No, thanks. Have you been here in your house for the last three days?"

I poured myself a glass of milk and took a big gulp. "Yeah. How about you?"

"I'm worried about you, Poppy. You weren't ready to see someone die right in front of you."

The concern in his deep brown eyes triggered something inside me, and I felt the tears begin again. Looking away, I tried to brush off his worry. "I've seen people die before, Alex. I saw my mother die, so it's nothing new to me."

I swallowed hard and willed the tears to go the hell away again, but they were stronger than I was this time and they came with a vengeance. Turning my back to him, I so wished I didn't look so weak and pathetic, but it was no use.

That's what I was. Not much of a hard-nosed detective like him, was I?

He put his arms around me and pulled me into him

as I sobbed like a baby over Dominick. Over Alicia. Over my mother too. I let it all out right there in my kitchen as Alex held me through the sobs and shudders, all the while saying nothing and just hugging me to him.

For nearly ten minutes, we stood like that, him helping me get through what we'd experienced and me unable to do much else than let it all out, as my father always said would make me feel better. It did, and when my tears had stopped, I wiped under my eyes and stepped back to look up at Alex waiting to see if I needed him again just in case the waterworks started once more.

"Thanks. I guess I needed that. Not much of a detective, am I?"

He gave me one of those slowly spreading smiles that reached all the way up to his eyes. "I think you have great instincts. You know that, though."

Sniffling, I joked, "That you think that or that I have them?"

"Both. Are you going to be okay?"

For the first time in three days, I could honestly answer yes. "I'm going to be fine. Thanks for the shoulder to cry on. Well, I guess it would be more correct to say chest to cry on."

"Anytime. Whatever body part you want to cry on."

I felt my cheeks flush with heat and knew I was blushing at his completely innocent comment. Embarrassed, I turned away to take another drink of milk so he wouldn't see my reaction.

"Well, I have to go. I have a meeting with Derek about some things."

I spun around. "You mean about the case?"

"Sort of. A few loose ends to tie up since the shooting did happen at my house. Nothing you have to worry about, though. Everything's solved, so it's all wrapped up."

"Oh. Okay."

I had to admit that now that I'd let out all those emotions I'd kept inside for the past few days, the idea of working on something cheered me up and hearing there was nothing else to do with the Geneva case disappointed me a little.

"Meet me at The Grounds tomorrow at nine like always?" he asked as he moved toward the door to leave.

"Sure, but you just said there's nothing more to do with the case."

He nodded and smiled again. "True, but we're more than just that case, aren't we? Friends and partners, right?"

"Right. Okay, I'll be there at nine."

"See you tomorrow, Poppy."

As I watched the door close behind him, I suddenly had a hunger for beef stew as only my father could make it. Trotting back to my phone, I called him and without even saying hello, I asked, "Is that offer for your world famous stew still open? I think I'm feeling up to it now."

"Of course! What changed your mind?" he asked, always curious about me.

"Just talked to a friend. That's all. See you in an hour, okay, Dad?"

"See you in an hour, Poppy."

AT FIVE MINUTES before nine the next morning, I took my seat at the back of The Grounds and waited for Alex. I'd spent a wonderful night with my father enjoying his beef stew and talking about a lot of things, especially my mother, and now I wanted to have a much needed coffee with my friend and partner. I fully intended on listening closely when he ordered his coffee so I knew how he took his morning drink like he knew mine. I had a lot to learn about investigating, and that was the first step I wanted to take.

The crowd at The Grounds filled up the shop quickly, so seeing the front door became impossible after just a few minutes. Sure he'd know to come to our usual seat, I scrolled through messages on my phone, deleting the ones from my former job at The Bottom Line.

"Dark roast the Poppy McGuire way, two sugars and extra cream," he said as he set our two cups down.

Deleting one last message, I said, "Oh, I wanted to hear how you get yours so I could know for the future."

I looked up from my phone and felt my eyes grow as wide as saucers. Standing there next to the table was Alex dressed in a navy blue Sunset Ridge policeman's uniform. It made him look bigger than he usually looked, and the color made his dark hair and eyes stand out like I'd never seen them before.

The effect was nothing less than stunning.

"What's…what's this?"

With a smile, he said as he sat down across from me, "This was what I had to go see Derek about last night. Since Dominick's death, the council made him chief, so Sunset Ridge needed a new officer. I guess my past experience was good enough because they offered me the job two days ago. Last night, I agreed to become the newest officer on the Sunset Ridge police force."

"I love it! I think you're going to be great, of course."

"I only said yes after they agreed to my one demand," he said with a sly grin.

"Better pay? I imagine they offered you peanuts, right? You have to shake these local guys down. A former Baltimore police detective doesn't come cheap, and they should know that."

He smiled and shook his head. "That wasn't my demand. I agreed to join the force only if they agreed that you would be working with me from now on."

My mouth dropped open as I sat there in shock. "Me? You want to keep working with me?"

"It's not every day I meet someone with such good instincts who knows the lay of the land, Poppy. Are you willing to keep solving crimes with me?"

Still stunned, I answered without even thinking. "Of course! I'm just so surprised."

"Derek said yes as soon as I mentioned it to him," he explained. He took a sip of his coffee and added, "But considering how much he likes you I knew he would."

"I'm just surprised you wanted to."

"It was my only demand. You're right, though. The pay is pretty bad. Thankfully, I have my pension from being a detective or I wouldn't be able to afford coffee and danish every morning."

I stood from the table to head up to the counter. "This is a celebration, so today's is my treat. Cherry or cheese?"

"Cherry sounds good."

Grinning from ear to ear at seeing him sitting there dressed like that and now my official partner, I said, "Two cherries it is."

After fielding twenty questions from Jennie and three women in line about who the very handsome police officer was sitting with me, I returned to our table and gave him his celebratory cherry danish. Lifting my coffee cup, I said, "To Alex Montero, the newest Sunset Ridge Police officer and my partner. Congratulations!"

As was his style, he smiled and nodded, but he said nothing before biting into his danish. I truly felt happier than I'd been in a long time. Alex had a new job that would keep him in the land of the living, and I had a new purpose.

"By the way, it's just regular coffee with two sugars and one cream," he said as he put his fork down after finishing his food.

"The way you take your coffee?"

"Yeah. I bet you thought it would be something far more exciting, but it's like everyone takes it. Sometimes when I really need the jolt from caffeine, I take it black. Pretty average."

I looked across the table and couldn't imagine Alex Montero ever being considered anything like average. I'd seen run-of-the-mill all my life in Sunset Ridge, and I knew he was nothing like anyone I'd ever met before.

"So are you ready for our next case?" he asked with a sparkle in his eyes.

"I'm more than ready. Lead the way!"

**Poppy and Alex return in After Hours:
A Poppy McGuire Mystery
(Poppy McGuire Mysteries #2)**

About The Author

Anina Collins has always loved a good mystery. From Agatha Christie's Hercule Poirot to Sir Arthur Conan Doyle's famous detective Sherlock Holmes to Dan Brown's intrepid Professor Robert Langdon, she's spent some of her favorite reading times with mystery novels. When she's not writing her favorite mystery couple, she can be found watching entirely too much Supernatural and dreaming about the beach.

Visit Anina's Facebook page at facebook.com/Anina-Collins-429334270597293 for news about her books, along with giveaways and other fun stuff!

And sign up for her newsletter today for exclusive news first! Visit her website at aninacollins.com for more details.

Books by Anina Collins:
The Eleventh Hour (Poppy McGuire Mysteries #1)
After Hours (Poppy McGuire Mysteries #2)
Top of the Hour (Poppy McGuire Mysteries #3)

And look for the next book in the series, **The Darkest Hour (Poppy McGuire Mysteries #4)**, coming JULY 2016!